GIRLS AT WAR AND OTHER STORIES

GIRLS AT WAR,

and other stories .

---

by Chinua Achebe

DOUBLEDAY & COMPANY, INC.
GARDEN CITY, NEW YORK
1973

GIRLS AT WAR AND OTHER STORIES was first published in 1972 by
Heinemann Educational Books Limited, London.

ISBN: 0-385-00852-X
Library of Congress Catalog Card Number 72–85361
Copyright © 1972, 1973 by Chinua Achebe
Printed in the United States of America

Acknowledgments

"The Madman" was first published in a shorter version in *The Insider* (Nwankwo-Ifejika), Enugu, 1971.

"The Voter" was first published in *Black Orpheus*, No. 17, 1965.

"Marriage Is a Private Affair" was first published under a different title in *The University Herald*, Ibadan, May 1952.

"Akueke" was first published in *Reflections* (Andre Deutsch), edited by Frances Ademola.

"Chike's School Days" was first published in *Rotarian*, April 1960.

"The Sacrificial Egg" was first published in a shorter version in *Atlantic Monthly*, April 1959.

"Vengeful Creditor" was first published in *Okike*, No. 1, 1971.

"Dead Men's Path" was first published in *The University Herald,* Ibadan, January 1953 (untitled).

"Uncle Ben's Choice" was first published in *Black Orpheus,* No. 19, 1966.

"Civil Peace" was first published in *Okike,* No. 2, 1971.

Contents

Preface

It was with something of a shock that I realized that my earliest short stories were published as long ago as twenty years in the Ibadan student magazine, *The University Herald*. I suppose I had come to think that that exciting adjective "new" so beloved of advertisers and salesmen would stick to me indefinitely. But alas a practitioner of twenty years standing should no longer be called new. All that he can do is probably to draw some comfort from looking at his art in the light of wine (which improves with age) rather than, say, detergent which has to be ever new. And I do not necessarily mean wine of the vine, for the palm-tree which I know better has its wine too, somewhat sweet when it is first brought down in the morning but harsher and more potent as the day advances.

I have felt another kind of disappointment in the fewness of the stories. A dozen pieces in twenty years must be accounted a pretty lean harvest by any reckoning. A countryman of mine once described himself as "a voracious writer." On my present showing I could not possibly make a similar claim. I do hope, however, that this little collection does have some merit and interest, even the two student pieces (I dare not call them stories) which I have slightly touched up here and there without, I hope, destroying their primal ingenuousness.

Another fellow countryman of mine, Wole Soyinka, once charged me, albeit in a friendly way, with an "unrelieved competence" in my novels. I trust that some at least of these short stories stretching farther back in time than the novels and touching upon more varied areas of experience will please by occasional departures into relieved competence (to say nothing of relieved and unrelieved incompetence).

I am grateful to Professors Thomas Melone of Yaoundé and G. D. Killam of Dar es Salaam for tracking down some of the earliest of these stories.

CHINUA ACHEBE

Institute of African Studies
University of Nigeria
Nsukka

GIRLS AT WAR AND OTHER STORIES

THE MADMAN

HE WAS drawn to markets and straight roads. Not any
tiny neighbourhood market where a handful of garru-
lous women might gather at sunset to gossip and buy
ogili for the evening's soup, but a huge, engulfing bazaar
beckoning people familiar and strange from far and
near. And not any dusty, old footpath beginning in this
village, and ending in that stream, but broad, black,
mysterious highways without beginning or end. After
much wandering he had discovered two such markets
linked together by such a highway; and so ended his
wandering. One market was Afo, the other Eke. The two
days between them suited him very well: before setting
out for Eke he had ample time to wind up his business
properly at Afo. He passed the night there putting right

again his hut after a day of defilement by two fat-bottomed market women who said it was their market-stall. At first he had put up a fight but the women had gone and brought their men-folk—four hefty beasts of the bush—to whip him out of the hut. After that he always avoided them, moving out on the morning of the market and back in at dusk to pass the night. Then in the morning he rounded off his affairs swiftly and set out on that long, beautiful boa-constrictor of a road to Eke in the distant town of Ogbu. He held his staff and cudgel at the ready in his right hand, and with the left he steadied the basket of his belongings on his head. He had got himself this cudgel lately to deal with little beasts on the way who threw stones at him and made fun of their mothers' nakedness, not his own.

He used to walk in the middle of the road, holding it in conversation. But one day the driver of a mammy-wagon and his mate came down on him shouting, pushing and slapping his face. They said their lorry very nearly ran over their mother, not him. After that he avoided those noisy lorries too, with the vagabonds inside them.

Having walked one day and one night he was now close to the Eke market-place. From every little side-road crowds of market people poured into the big highway to join the enormous flow to Eke. Then he saw some young ladies with water-pots on their heads coming towards him, unlike all the rest, away from the market. This surprised him. Then he saw two more water-pots rise out of a sloping footpath leading off his side of the highway. He felt thirsty then and stopped to think it over.

Then he set down his basket on the roadside and turned into the sloping footpath. But first he begged his highway not to be offended or continue the journey without him. "I'll get some for you too," he said coaxingly with a tender backward glance. "I know you are thirsty."

Nwibe was a man of high standing in Ogbu and was rising higher; a man of wealth and integrity. He had just given notice to all the ozo men of the town that he proposed to seek admission into their honoured hierarchy in the coming initiation season.

"Your proposal is excellent," said the men of title. "When we see we shall believe." Which was their dignified way of telling you to think it over once again and make sure you have the means to go through with it. For ozo is not a child's naming ceremony; and where is the man to hide his face who begins the ozo dance and then is foot-stuck to the arena? But in this instance the caution of the elders was no more than a formality for Nwibe was such a sensible man that no one could think of him beginning something he was not sure to finish.

On that Eke day Nwibe had risen early so as to visit his farm beyond the stream and do some light work before going to the market at midday to drink a horn or two of palm-wine with his peers and perhaps buy that bundle of roofing thatch for the repair of his wives' huts. As for his own hut he had a couple of years back settled it finally by changing his thatch-roof to zinc. Sooner or later he would do the same for his wives. He could have done Mgboye's hut right away but decided to wait until

he could do the two together, or else Udenkwo would
set the entire compound on fire. Udenkwo was the junior
wife, by three years, but she never let that worry her.
Happily Mgboye was a woman of peace who rarely demanded the respect due to her from the other. She would
suffer Udenkwo's provoking tongue sometimes for a
whole day without offering a word in reply. And when
she did reply at all her words were always few and her
voice low.

That very morning Udenkwo had accused her of spite
and all kinds of wickedness on account of a little dog.

"What has a little dog done to you?" she screamed
loud enough for half the village to hear. "I ask you,
Mgboye, what is the offence of a puppy this early in the
day?"

"What your puppy did this early in the day," replied
Mgboye, "is that he put his shit-mouth into my soup-pot."

"And then?"

"And then I smacked him."

"You smacked him! Why don't you cover your soup-
pot? Is it easier to hit a dog than cover a pot? Is a small
puppy to have more sense than a woman who leaves her
soup-pot about . . . ?"

"Enough from you, Udenkwo."

"It is not enough, Mgboye, it is not enough. If that
dog owes you any debt I want to know. Everything I
have, even a little dog I bought to eat my infant's ex-
crement keeps you awake at nights. You are a bad
woman, Mgboye, you are a very bad woman!"

Nwibe had listened to all of this in silence in his hut.
He knew from the vigour in Udenkwo's voice that she

could go on like this till market-time. So he intervened, in his characteristic manner by calling out to his senior wife.

"Mgboye! Let me have peace this early morning!"

"Don't you hear all the abuses Udenkwo . . ."

"I hear nothing at all from Udenkwo and I want peace in my compound. If Udenkwo is crazy must everybody else go crazy with her? Is one crazy woman not enough in my compound so early in the day?"

"The great judge has spoken," sang Udenkwo in a sneering sing-song. "Thank you, great judge. Udenkwo is mad. Udenkwo is always mad, but those of you who are sane let . . ."

"Shut your mouth, shameless woman, or a wild beast will lick your eyes for you this morning. When will you learn to keep your badness within this compound instead of shouting it to all Ogbu to hear? I say shut your mouth!"

There was silence then except for Udenkwo's infant whose yelling had up till then been swallowed up by the larger noise of the adults.

"Don't cry, my father," sang Udenkwo to him. "They want to kill your dog, but our people say the man who decides to chase after a chicken, for him is the fall . . ."

By the middle of the morning Nwibe had done all the work he had to do on his farm and was on his way again to prepare for market. At the little stream he decided as he always did to wash off the sweat of work. So he put his cloth on a huge boulder by the men's bathing section and waded in. There was nobody else around because of the time of day and because it was market day. But from

instinctive modesty he turned to face the forest away
from the approaches.

The madman watched him for quite a while. Each time
he bent down to carry water in cupped hands from the
shallow stream to his head and body the madman smiled
at his parted behind. And then remembered. This was
the same hefty man who brought three others like him
and whipped me out of my hut in the Afo market. He
nodded to himself. And he remembered again: this was
the same vagabond who descended on me from the lorry
in the middle of my highway. He nodded once more.
And then he remembered yet again: this was the same
fellow who set his children to throw stones at me and
make remarks about their mothers' buttocks, not mine.
Then he laughed.

Nwibe turned sharply round and saw the naked man
laughing, the deep grove of the stream amplifying his
laughter. Then he stopped as suddenly as he had begun;
the merriment vanished from his face.

"I have caught you naked," he said.

Nwibe ran a hand swiftly down his face to clear his
eyes of water.

"I say I have caught you naked, with your thing dan-
gling about."

"I can see you are hungry for a whipping," said Nwibe
with quiet menace in his voice, for a madman is said to
be easily scared away by the very mention of a whip.
"Wait till I get up there. . . . What are you doing?
Drop it at once . . . I say drop it!"

The madman had picked up Nwibe's cloth and

wrapped it round his own waist. He looked down at himself and began to laugh again.

"I will kill you," screamed Nwibe as he splashed towards the bank, maddened by anger. "I will whip that madness out of you today!"

They ran all the way up the steep and rocky footpath hedged in by the shadowy green forest. A mist gathered and hung over Nwibe's vision as he ran, stumbled, fell, pulled himself up again and stumbled on, shouting and cursing. The other, despite his unaccustomed encumbrance steadily increased his lead, for he was spare and wiry, a thing made for speed. Furthermore, he did not waste his breath shouting and cursing; he just ran. Two girls going down to the stream saw a man running up the slope towards them pursued by a stark-naked madman. They threw down their pots and fled, screaming.

When Nwibe emerged into the full glare of the highway he could not see his cloth clearly any more and his chest was on the point of exploding from the fire and torment within. But he kept running. He was only vaguely aware of crowds of people on all sides and he appealed to them tearfully without stopping: "Hold the madman, he's got my cloth!" By this time the man with the cloth was practically lost among the much denser crowds far in front so that the link between him and the naked man was no longer clear.

Now Nwibe continually bumped against people's backs and then laid flat a frail old man struggling with a stubborn goat on a leash. "Stop the madman," he shouted hoarsely, his heart tearing to shreds, "he's got my cloth!" Everyone looked at him first in surprise and then less

surprise because strange sights are common in a great
market. Some of them even laughed.

"They've got his cloth he says."

"That's a new one I'm sure. He hardly looks mad yet.
Doesn't he have people, I wonder."

"People are so careless these days. Why can't they keep
proper watch over their sick relation, especially on the
day of the market?"

Farther up the road on the very brink of the market-place
two men from Nwibe's village recognized him and,
throwing down the one his long basket of yams, the other
his calabash of palm-wine held on a loop, gave desperate
chase, to stop him setting foot irrevocably within the
occult territory of the powers of the market. But it was
in vain. When finally they caught him it was well inside
the crowded square. Udenkwo in tears tore off her top-
cloth which they draped on him and led him home by
the hand. He spoke just once about a madman who took
his cloth in the stream.

"It is all right," said one of the men in the tone of a
father to a crying child. They led and he followed
blindly, his heavy chest heaving up and down in silent
weeping. Many more people from his village, a few of
his in-laws and one or two others from his mother's place
had joined the grief-stricken party. One man whispered
to another that it was the worst kind of madness, deep
and tongue-tied.

"May it end ill for him who did this," prayed the other.

The first medicine-man his relatives consulted refused
to take him on, out of some kind of integrity.

"I could say yes to you and take your money," he said. "But that is not my way. My powers of cure are known throughout Olu and Igbo but never have I professed to bring back to life a man who has sipped the spirit-waters of ani-mmọ. It is the same with a madman who of his own accord delivers himself to the divinities of the market-place. You should have kept better watch over him."

"Don't blame us too much," said Nwibe's relative. "When he left home that morning his senses were as complete as yours and mine now. Don't blame us too much."

"Yes, I know. It happens that way sometimes. And they are the ones that medicine will not reach. I know."

"Can you do nothing at all then, not even to untie his tongue?"

"Nothing can be done. They have already embraced him. It is like a man who runs away from the oppression of his fellows to the grove of an alusi and says to him: Take me, oh spirit, I am your osu. No man can touch him thereafter. He is free and yet no power can break his bondage. He is free of men but bonded to a god."

The second doctor was not as famous as the first and not so strict. He said the case was bad, very bad indeed, but no one folds his arms because the condition of his child is beyond hope. He must still grope around and do his best. His hearers nodded in eager agreement. And then he muttered into his own inward ear: If doctors were to send away every patient whose cure they were uncertain of, how many of them would eat one meal in a whole week from their practice?

Nwibe was cured of his madness. That humble prac-

titioner who did the miracle became overnight the most
celebrated mad-doctor of his generation. They called him
Sojourner to the Land of the Spirits. Even so it remains
true that madness may indeed sometimes depart but
never with all his clamorous train. Some of these always
remain—the trailers of madness you might call them—to
haunt the doorway of the eyes. For how could a man be
the same again of whom witnesses from all the lands
of Olu and Igbo have once reported that they saw today
a fine, hefty man in his prime, stark naked, tearing
through the crowds to answer the call of the market-
place? Such a man is marked for ever.

Nwibe became a quiet, withdrawn man avoiding whenever he could the boisterous side of the life of his people.
Two years later, before another initiation season, he
made a new inquiry about joining the community of
titled men in his town. Had they received him perhaps
he might have become at least partially restored, but
those ozo men, dignified and polite as ever, deftly steered
the conversation away to other matters.

THE VOTER

Rufus Okeke—Roof for short—was a very popular man in his village. Although the villagers did not explain it in so many words Roof's popularity was a measure of their gratitude to an energetic young man who, unlike most of his fellows nowadays had not abandoned the village in order to seek work, any work, in the towns. And Roof was not a village lout either. Everyone knew how he had spent two years as a bicycle repairer's apprentice in Port Harcourt, and had given up of his own free will a bright future to return to his people and guide them in these difficult times. Not that Umuofia needed a lot of guidance. The village already belonged *en masse* to the People's Alliance Party, and its most illustrious son, Chief the Honourable Marcus Ibe, was Minister of Cul-

ture in the outgoing government (which was pretty certain to be the in-coming one as well). Nobody doubted
that the Honourable Minister would be elected in his
constituency. Opposition to him was like the proverbial
fly trying to move a dunghill. It would have been
ridiculous enough without coming, as it did now, from
a complete nonentity.

As was to be expected Roof was in the service of the
Honourable Minister for the coming elections. He had
become a real expert in election campaigning at all
levels—village, local government or national. He could
tell the mood and temper of the electorate at any given
time. For instance he had warned the Minister months
ago about the radical change that had come into the
thinking of Umuofia since the last national election.

_ The villagers had had five years in which to see how
quickly and plentifully politics brought wealth, chief-
taincy titles, doctorate degrees and other honours some
of which, like the last, had still to be explained satisfac-
torily to them; for in their naïvety they still expected a
doctor to be able to heal the sick.´ Anyhow, these honours and benefits had come so readily to the man to
whom they had given their votes free of charge five years
ago that they were now ready to try it a different way.

Their point was that only the other day Marcus Ibe
was a not too successful mission school teacher. Then
politics had come to their village and he had wisely
joined up, some said just in time to avoid imminent dis-
missal arising from a female teacher's pregnancy. Today
he was Chief the Honourable; he had two long cars and
had just built himself the biggest house anyone had seen

in these parts. But let it be said that none of these successes had gone to Marcus's head as well they might. He remained devoted to his people. Whenever he could he left the good things of the capital and returned to his village which had neither running water nor electricity, although he had lately installed a private plant to supply electricity to his new house. He knew the source of his good fortune, unlike the little bird who ate and drank and went out to challenge his personal spirit. Marcus had christened his new house "Umuofia Mansions" in honour of his village, and he had slaughtered five bulls and countless goats to entertain the people on the day it was opened by the Archbishop.

Every one was full of praise for him. One old man said: "Our son is a good man; he is not like the mortar which as soon as food comes its way turns its back on the ground." But when the feasting was over, the villagers told themselves that they had underrated the power of the ballot paper before and should not do so again. Chief the Honourable Marcus Ibe was not unprepared. He had drawn five months' salary in advance, changed a few hundred pounds into shining shillings and armed his campaign boys with eloquent little jute bags. In the day he made his speeches; at night his stalwarts conducted their whispering campaign. Roof was the most trusted of these campaigners.

"We have a Minister from our village, one of our own sons," he said to a group of elders in the house of Ogbuefi Ezenwa, a man of high traditional title. "What greater honour can a village have? Do you ever stop to ask yourselves why we should be singled out for this honour? I

will tell you; it is because we are favoured by the leaders of PAP. Whether or not we cast our paper for Marcus,
PAP will continue to rule. Think of the pipe-borne water
they have promised us . . ."

Besides Roof and his assistant there were five elders
in the room. An old hurricane lamp with a cracked, sooty,
glass chimney gave out yellowish light in their midst.
The elders sat on very low stools. On the floor, directly
in front of each of them, lay two shilling pieces. Outside
beyond the fastened door, the moon kept a straight face.

"We believe every word you say to be true," said
Ezenwa. "We shall, every one of us, drop his paper for
Marcus. Who would leave an ozo feast and go to a poor
ritual meal? Tell Marcus he has our papers, and our
wives' papers too. But what we do say is that two shillings
is shameful." He brought the lamp close and tilted it at
the money before him as if to make sure he had not mis-
taken its value. "Yes, two shillings is too shameful. If
Marcus were a poor man—which our ancestors forbid—I
should be the first to give him my paper free, as I did
before. But today Marcus is a great man and does his
things like a great man. We did not ask him for money
yesterday; we shall not ask him tomorrow. But today is
our day; we have climbed the iroko tree today and would
be foolish not to take down all the firewood we need."

Roof had to agree. He had lately been taking down
a lot of firewood himself. Only yesterday he had asked
Marcus for one of his many rich robes—and had got it.
Last Sunday Marcus's wife (the teacher that nearly got
him in trouble) had objected (like the woman she was)
when Roof pulled out his fifth bottle of beer from the

refrigerator; she was roundly and publicly rebuked by
her husband. To cap it all Roof had won a land case recently because, among other things, he had been
chauffeur-driven to the disputed site. So he understood
the elders about the firewood.

"All right," he said in English and then reverted to
Ibo. "Let us not quarrel about small things." He stood
up, adjusted his robes and plunged his hand once more
into the bag. Then he bent down like a priest distributing
the host and gave one shilling more to every man; only
he did not put it into their palms but on the floor in
front of them. The men, who had so far not deigned to
touch the things, looked at the floor and shook their
heads. Roof got up again and gave each man another
shilling.

"I am through," he said with a defiance that was no
less effective for being transparently faked. The elders
too knew how far to go without losing decorum. So
when Roof added: "Go cast your paper for the enemy
if you like!" they quickly calmed him down with a suit-
able speech from each of them. By the time the last man
had spoken it was possible, without great loss of dignity,
to pick up the things from the floor . . .

The enemy Roof had referred to was the Progressive
Organization Party (POP) which had been formed by
the tribes down the coast to save themselves, as the
founders of the party proclaimed, from "total political,
cultural, social and religious annihilation." Although it
was clear the party had no chance here it had plunged,
with typical foolishness, into a straight fight with PAP,

providing cars and loud-speakers to a few local rascals
and thugs to go around and make a lot of noise. No one
knew for certain how much money POP had let loose
in Umuofia but it was said to be very considerable. Their
local campaigners would end up very rich, no doubt.

Up to last night everything had been "moving according to plan," as Roof would have put it. Then he had received a strange visit from the leader of the POP campaign team. Although he and Roof were well known to
each other, and might even be called friends, his visit
was cold and business-like. No words were wasted. He
placed five pounds on the floor before Roof and said, "We
want your vote." Roof got up from his chair, went to the
outside door, closed it carefully and returned to his chair.
The brief exercise gave him enough time to weigh the
proposition. As he spoke his eyes never left the red notes
on the floor. He seemed to be mesmerized by the picture of the cocoa farmer harvesting his crops.

"You know I work for Marcus," he said feebly. "It will
be very bad . . ."

"Marcus will not be there when you put in your paper.
We have plenty of work to do tonight; are you taking
this or not?"

"It will not be heard outside this room?" asked Roof.

"We are after votes not gossip."

"All right," said Roof in English.

The man nudged his companion and he brought forward an object covered with a red cloth and proceeded
to remove the cover. It was a fearsome little affair con-
tained in a clay pot with feathers stuck into it.

"The *iyi* comes from Mbanta. You know what that

means. Swear that you will vote for Maduka. If you fail
to do so, this *iyi* take note."

Roof's heart nearly flew out when he saw the *iyi;* indeed he knew the fame of Mbanta in these things. But
he was a man of quick decision. What could a single vote
cast in secret for Maduka take away from Marcus's certain victory? Nothing.

"I will cast my paper for Maduka; if not this *iyi* take
note."

"Das all," said the man as he rose with his companion
who had covered up the object again and was taking it
back to their car.

"You know he has no chance against Marcus," said
Roof at the door.

"It is enough that he gets a few votes now; next time
he will get more. People will hear that he gives out
pounds, not shillings, and they will listen."

Election morning. The great day every five years when
the people exercise power. Weather-beaten posters on
walls of houses, tree trunks and telegraph poles. The few
that were still whole called out their message to those
who could read. Vote for the People's Alliance Party!
Vote for the Progressive Organization Party! Vote for
PAP! Vote for POP! The posters that were torn called out
as much of the message as they could.

As usual Chief the Honourable Marcus Ibe was doing
things in grand style. He had hired a highlife band from
Umuru and stationed it at such a distance from the vot-
ing booths as just managed to be lawful. Many villagers
danced to the music, their ballot papers held aloft, be-

fore proceeding to the booths. Chief the Honourable
Marcus Ibe sat in the "owner's corner" of his enormous
green car and smiled and nodded. One enlightened vil-
lager came up to the car, shook hands with the great
man and said in advance, "Congrats!" This immediately
set the pattern. Hundreds of admirers shook Marcus's
hand and said "Corngrass!"

Roof and the other organizers were prancing up and
down, giving last minute advice to the voters and pour-
ing with sweat.

"Do not forget," he said again to a group of illiterate
women who seemed ready to burst with enthusiasm and
good humour, "our sign is the motor-car . . ."

"Like the one Marcus is sitting inside."

"Thank you, mother," said Roof. "It is the same car.
The box with the car shown on its body is the box for
you. Don't look at the other with the man's head: it
is for those whose heads are not correct."

This was greeted with loud laughter. Roof cast a quick
and busy-like glance towards the Minister and received
a smile of appreciation.

"Vote for the car," he shouted, all the veins in his neck
standing out. "Vote for the car and you will ride in it!"

"Or if we don't, our children will," piped the same
sharp, old girl.

The band struck up a new number: "Why walk when
you can ride . . ."

In spite of his apparent calm and confidence Chief the
Honourable Marcus was a relentless stickler for detail.
He knew he would win what the newspapers called "a
landslide victory" but he did not wish, even so, to throw

away a single vote. So as soon as the first rush of voters was over he promptly asked his campaign boys to go one at a time and put in their ballot papers.

"Roof, you had better go first," he said.

Roof's spirits fell; but he let no one see it. All morning he had masked his deep worry with a surface exertion which was unusual even for him. Now he dashed off in his springy fashion towards the booths. A policeman at the entrance searched him for illegal ballot papers and passed him. Then the electoral officer explained to him about the two boxes. By this time the spring had gone clean out of his walk. He sidled in and was confronted by the car and the head. He brought out his ballot paper from his pocket and looked at it. How could he betray Marcus even in secret? He resolved to go back to the other man and return his five pounds . . . Five pounds! He knew at once it was impossible. He had sworn on that *iyi*. The notes were red; the cocoa farmer busy at work.

At this point he heard the muffled voice of the policeman asking the electoral officer what the man was doing inside. "Abi na pickin im de born?"

Quick as lightning a thought leapt into Roof's mind. He folded the paper, tore it in two along the crease and put one half in each box. He took the precaution of putting the first half into Maduka's box and confirming the action verbally: "I vote for Maduka."

They marked his thumb with indelible purple ink to prevent his return, and he went out of the booth as jauntily as he had gone in.

MARRIAGE IS A
PRIVATE AFFAIR

"Have you written to your dad yet?" asked Nene one afternoon as she sat with Nnaemeka in her room at 16 Kasanga Street, Lagos.

"No. I've been thinking about it. I think it's better to tell him when I get home on leave!"

"But why? Your leave is such a long way off yet—six whole weeks. He should be let into our happiness now."

Nnaemeka was silent for a while, and then began very slowly as if he groped for his words: "I wish I were sure it would be happiness to him."

"Of course it must," replied Nene, a little surprised. "Why shouldn't it?"

"You have lived in Lagos all your life, and you know very little about people in remote parts of the country."

"That's what you always say. But I don't believe anybody will be so unlike other people that they will be unhappy when their sons are engaged to marry."

"Yes. They are most unhappy if the engagement is not arranged by them. In our case it's worse—you are not even an Ibo."

This was said so seriously and so bluntly that Nene could not find speech immediately. In the cosmopolitan atmosphere of the city it had always seemed to her something of a joke that a person's tribe could determine whom he married.

At last she said, "You don't really mean that he will object to your marrying me simply on that account? I had always thought you Ibos were kindly-disposed to other people."

"So we are. But when it comes to marriage, well, it's not quite so simple. And this," he added, "is not peculiar to the Ibos. If your father were alive and lived in the heart of Ibibio-land he would be exactly like my father."

"I don't know. But anyway, as your father is so fond of you, I'm sure he will forgive you soon enough. Come on then, be a good boy and send him a nice lovely letter . . ."

"It would not be wise to break the news to him by writing. A letter will bring it upon him with a shock. I'm quite sure about that."

"All right, honey, suit yourself. You know your father."

As Nnaemeka walked home that evening he turned over in his mind different ways of overcoming his father's opposition, especially now that he had gone and found a girl for him. He had thought of showing his letter to Nene but decided on second thoughts not to, at least for the moment. He read it again when he got home and couldn't help smiling to himself. He remembered Ugoye quite well, an Amazon of a girl who used to beat up all the boys, himself included, on the way to the stream, a complete dunce at school.

I have found a girl who will suit you admirably— Ugoye Nweke, the eldest daughter of our neighbour, Jacob Nweke. She has a proper Christian upbringing. When she stopped schooling some years ago her father (a man of sound judgement) sent her to live in the house of a pastor where she has received all the training a wife could need. Her Sunday School teacher has told me that she reads her Bible very fluently. I hope we shall begin negotiations when you come home in December.

On the second evening of his return from Lagos Nnaemeka sat with his father under a cassia tree. This was the old man's retreat where he went to read his Bible when the parching December sun had set and a fresh, reviving wind blew on the leaves.

"Father," began Nnaemeka suddenly, "I have come to ask for forgiveness."

"Forgiveness? For what, my son?" he asked in amazement.

"It's about this marriage question."

"Which marriage question?"

"I can't—we must—I mean it is impossible for me to marry Nweke's daughter."

"Impossible? Why?" asked his father.

"I don't love her."

"Nobody said you did. Why should you?" he asked.

"Marriage today is different . . ."

"Look here, my son," interrupted his father, "nothing is different. What one looks for in a wife are a good character and a Christian background."

Nnaemeka saw there was no hope along the present line of argument.

"Moreover," he said, "I am engaged to marry another girl who has all of Ugoye's good qualities, and who . . ."

His father did not believe his ears. "What did you say?" he asked slowly and disconcertingly.

"She is a good Christian," his son went on, "and a teacher in a Girls' School in Lagos."

"Teacher, did you say? If you consider that a qualification for a good wife I should like to point out to you, Emeka, that no Christian woman should teach. St. Paul in his letter to the Corinthians says that women should keep silence." He rose slowly from his seat and paced forwards and backwards. This was his pet subject, and he condemned vehemently those church leaders who encouraged women to teach in their schools. After he had spent his emotion on a long homily he at last came back to his son's engagement, in a seemingly milder tone.

"Whose daughter is she, anyway?"

"She is Nene Atang."

"What!" All the mildness was gone again. "Did you say Neneataga, what does that mean?"

"Nene Atang from Calabar. She is the only girl I can marry." This was a very rash reply and Nnaemeka expected the storm to burst. But it did not. His father

merely walked away into his room. This was most unexpected and perplexed Nnaemeka. His father's silence
was infinitely more menacing than a flood of threatening
speech. That night the old man did not eat.

When he sent for Nnaemeka a day later he applied
all possible ways of dissuasion. But the young man's heart
was hardened, and his father eventually gave him up as
lost.

"I owe it to you, my son, as a duty to show you what
is right and what is wrong. Whoever put this idea into
your head might as well have cut your throat. It is
Satan's work." He waved his son away.

"You will change your mind, Father, when you know
Nene."

"I shall never see her," was the reply. From that night
the father scarcely spoke to his son. He did not, however,
cease hoping that he would realize how serious was the
danger he was heading for. Day and night he put him in
his prayers.

Nnaemeka, for his own part, was very deeply affected
by his father's grief. But he kept hoping that it would pass
away. If it had occurred to him that never in the history
of his people had a man married a woman who spoke a
different tongue, he might have been less optimistic. "It
has never been heard," was the verdict of an old man
speaking a few weeks later. In that short sentence he
spoke for all of his people. This man had come with
others to commiserate with Okeke when news went
round about his son's behaviour. By that time the son
had gone back to Lagos.

"It has never been heard," said the old man again with a sad shake of his head.

"What did Our Lord say?" asked another gentleman. "Sons shall rise against their Fathers; it is there in the Holy Book."

"It is the beginning of the end," said another.

The discussion thus tending to become theological, Madubogwu, a highly practical man, brought it down once more to the ordinary level.

"Have you thought of consulting a native doctor about your son?" he asked Nnaemeka's father.

"He isn't sick," was the reply.

"What is he then? The boy's mind is diseased and only a good herbalist can bring him back to his right senses. The medicine he requires is *Amalile*, the same that women apply with success to recapture their husbands' straying affection."

"Madubogwu is right," said another gentleman. "This thing calls for medicine."

"I shall not call in a native doctor." Nnaemeka's father was known to be obstinately ahead of his more superstitious neighbours in these matters. "I will not be another Mrs. Ochuba. If my son wants to kill himself let him do it with his own hands. It is not for me to help him."

"But it was her fault," said Madubogwu. "She ought to have gone to an honest herbalist. She was a clever woman, nevertheless."

"She was a wicked murderess," said Jonathan who rarely argued with his neighbours because, he often said, they were incapable of reasoning. "The medicine was prepared for her husband, it was his name they called in its preparation and I am sure it would have been perfectly beneficial to him. It was wicked to put it into the herbalist's food, and say you were only trying it out."

Six months later, Nnaemeka was showing his young wife a short letter from his father:

> It amazes me that you could be so unfeeling as to send me your wedding picture. I would have sent it back. But on further thought I decided just to cut off your wife and send it back to you because I have nothing to do with her. How I wish that I had nothing to do with you either.

When Nene read through this letter and looked at the mutilated picture her eyes filled with tears, and she began to sob.

"Don't cry, my darling," said her husband. "He is essentially good-natured and will one day look more kindly on our marriage." But years passed and that one day did not come.

For eight years, Okeke would have nothing to do with his son, Nnaemeka. Only three times (when Nnaemeka asked to come home and spend his leave) did he write to him.

"I can't have you in my house," he replied on one occasion. "It can be of no interest to me where or how you spend your leave—or your life, for that matter."

The prejudice against Nnaemeka's marriage was not confined to his little village. In Lagos, especially among his people who worked there, it showed itself in a different way. Their women, when they met at their village

meeting, were not hostile to Nene. Rather, they paid her
such excessive deference as to make her feel she was not
one of them. But as time went on, Nene gradually broke
through some of this prejudice and even began to make
friends among them. Slowly and grudgingly they began
to admit that she kept her home much better than most
of them.

The story eventually got to the little village in the heart
of the Ibo country that Nnaemeka and his young wife
were a most happy couple. But his father was one of the
few people in the village who knew nothing about this.
He always displayed so much temper whenever his son's
name was mentioned that everyone avoided it in his
presence. By a tremendous effort of will he had succeeded in pushing his son to the back of his mind. The
strain had nearly killed him but he had persevered, and
won.

Then one day he received a letter from Nene, and in
spite of himself he began to glance through it perfunc-
torily until all of a sudden the expression on his face
changed and he began to read more carefully.

> . . . Our two sons, from the day they learnt that they
> have a grandfather, have insisted on being taken to
> him. I find it impossible to tell them that you will not
> see them. I implore you to allow Nnaemeka to bring
> them home for a short time during his leave next
> month. I shall remain here in Lagos . . .

The old man at once felt the resolution he had built up
over so many years falling in. He was telling himself that

he must not give in. He tried to steel his heart against all emotional appeals. It was a re-enactment of that other struggle. He leaned against a window and looked out. The sky was overcast with heavy black clouds and a high wind began to blow filling the air with dust and dry leaves. It was one of those rare occasions when even Nature takes a hand in a human fight. Very soon it began to rain, the first rain in the year. It came down in large sharp drops and was accompanied by the lightning and thunder which mark a change of season. Okeke was trying hard not to think of his two grandsons. But he knew he was now fighting a losing battle. He tried to hum a favourite hymn but the pattering of large rain drops on the roof broke up the tune. His mind immediately returned to the children. How could he shut his door against them? By a curious mental process he imagined them standing, sad and forsaken, under the harsh angry weather—shut out from his house.

That night he hardly slept, from remorse—and a vague fear that he might die without making it up to them.

AKUEKE

AKUEKE lay on her sick-bed on one side of the wall of enmity that had suddenly risen between her and her brothers. She heard their muttering with fear. They had not yet told her what must be done, but she knew. She wanted to ask them to take her to their mother's father in Ezi but so great was the enmity that had so strangely come between them that her pride forbade her to speak. Let them dare. Last night Ofodile who was the eldest had wanted to speak but had only stood and looked at her with tears in his eyes. Who was he crying for? Let him go and eat shit.

In the fitful half-sleep that later visited her Akueke was far away in her grandfather's compound in Ezi without even the memory of her sickness. She was once again the village beauty.

Akueke had been her mother's youngest child and only daughter. There were six brothers and their father had died when she was still a little girl. But he had been a man of substance so that even after his death his family did not know real want, especially as some of his sons already planted their own farms.

Several times every year Akueke's mother took her children to visit her own kinsmen in Ezi, a whole day's journey from Umuofia at the younger children's pace. Sometimes Akueke rode on her mother's back, sometimes she walked. When the sun came up her mother broke a little cassava twig from the roadside farm to protect her head.

Akueke looked forward to these visits to her mother's father, a giant of a man with white hair and beard. Sometimes the old man wore his beard as a rope-like plait ending in a fine point from which palm-wine dripped to the ground when he drank. This never ceased to amuse Akueke. The old man knew it and improved the situation for her by gnashing his teeth between gulps of wine.

He was very fond of his granddaughter who, they said, was the image of his own mother. He rarely called Akueke by her name: it was always *Mother*. She was in fact the older woman returned in the cycle of life. During the visits to Ezi, Akueke knew she could get away with anything; her grandfather forbade any one to rebuke her.

The voices beyond the wall grew louder. Perhaps neighbours were remonstrating with her brothers. So they all knew now. Let them all eat shit. If she could get up she would chase them all out with the old broom lying

near her bed. She wished her mother were alive. This
would not have happened to her.

Akueke's mother had died two years ago and was taken
to Ezi to be buried with her own people. The old man
who had seen many sorrows in his life asked, "Why do
they take my children and leave me?" But some days
later he told people who came to console him, "We are
God's chicken. Sometimes He chooses a young chicken
to eat and sometimes He chooses an old one." Akueke
remembered these scenes vividly and for once came
near to crying. What would the old man do when he
heard of her abominable death?

Akueke's age-grade brought out their first public dance
in the dry season that followed her mother's death.
Akueke created a sensation by her dancing, and her suit-
ors increased ten-fold. From one market to another some
man brought palm-wine to her brothers. But Akueke rejected them all. Her brothers began to be worried. They
all loved their only sister, and especially since their
mother's death, they seemed to vie with one another in
seeking her happiness.

And now they were worried because she was throwing
away chances of a good marriage. Her eldest brother,
Ofodile, told her as sternly as he could that proud girls
who refused every suitor often came to grief, like On-
wuero in the story, who rejected every man but in the
end ran after three fishes which had taken the form of
handsome young men in order to destroy her.

Akueke did not listen. And now her protective spirit
despairing of her had taken a hand in the matter and she

was stricken with this disease. At first people pretended
not to notice the swelling stomach.

Medicine men were brought in from far and wide to
minister to her. But their herbs and roots had no ef-
fect. An *afa* oracle sent Akueke's brothers in search of a
certain palm-tree smothered by a climbing vine. "When
you see it," he said to them, "take a matchet and cut away
the strangling climber. The spirits which have bound your
sister will then release her." The brothers searched
Umuofia and the neighbouring villages for three days before they saw such a palm-tree and cut it loose. But
their sister was not released; rather she got worse.

At last they took counsel together and decided with
heavy hearts that Akueke had been stricken with the
swelling disease which was an abomination to the land.
Akueke knew the purpose of her brothers' consultation.
As soon as the eldest set foot in her sick-room she began
to scream at him, and he fled. This went on for a whole
day, and there was a real danger that she might die in
the house and bring down the anger of *Ani* on the whole
family, if not the entire village. Neighbours came in and
warned the brothers of the grave danger to which they
were exposing the nine villages of Umuofia.

In the evening they carried her into the bad bush. They
had constructed a temporary shelter and a rough bed for
her. She was now silent from exhaustion and hate and
they left her and went away.

In the morning three of the brothers went again to the
bush to see whether she was still alive. To their great
shock the shelter was empty. They ran all the way back
to report to the others, and they all returned and began

a search of the bush. There was no sign of their sister. Obviously she had been eaten by wild animals, which sometimes happened in such cases.

Two or three moons passed and their grandfather sent a messenger to Umuofia to ascertain whether it was true that Akueke was dead. The brothers said "Yes" and the messenger returned to Ezi. A week or two later the old man sent another message commanding all the brothers to come to see him. He was waiting in his *obi* when his grandchildren arrived. After the formalities of welcome muted by thoughts of their recent loss he asked them where their sister was. The eldest told him the story of Akueke's death. The old man listened to the end with his head supported on the palm of his right hand.

"So Akueke is dead," he said, half question, half statement. "And why did you not send a message to me?" There was silence, then the eldest said they had wanted to complete all the purification rites. The old man gnashed his teeth, and then rose painfully three-quarters erect and tottered towards his sleeping-room, moved back the carved door and the ghost of Akueke stood before them, unsmiling and implacable. Everyone sprang to their feet and one or two were already outside.

"Come back," said the old man with a sad smile. "Do you know who this young woman is? I want an answer. You Ofodile, you are the eldest, I want you to answer. Who is this?"

"She is our sister Akueke."

"Your sister Akueke? But you have just told me that she died of the swelling disease. How could she die and then

be here?" Silence. "If you don't know what the swelling
disease is why did you not ask those who do?"

"We consulted medicine men throughout Umuofia and
Abame."

"Why did you not bring her here to me?" Silence.

The old man then said in very few words that
he had called them together to tell them that from that
day Akueke was to become his daughter and her name
would become Matefi. She was no longer a daughter of
Umuofia but of Ezi. They stared before them in silence.

"When she marries," the old man concluded, "her
bride-price will be mine not yours. As for your purification rites you may carry on because Akueke is truly dead
in Umuofia."

Without even a word of greeting to her brothers
Matefi went back to the room.

CHIKE'S SCHOOL DAYS

SARAH'S LAST CHILD was a boy, and his birth brought great joy to the house of his father, Amos. The child received three names at his baptism—John, Chike, Obiajulu. The last name means "the mind at last is at rest." Anyone hearing this name knew at once that its owner was either an only child or an only son. Chike was an only son. His parents had had five daughters before him.

Like his sisters Chike was brought up "in the ways of the white man," which meant the opposite of traditional. Amos had many years before bought a tiny bell with which he summoned his family to prayers and hymn-singing first thing in the morning and last thing at night. This was one of the ways of the white man. Sarah taught her children not to eat in their neighbours' houses be-

cause "they offered their food to idols." And thus she set
herself against the age-old custom which regarded children as the common responsibility of all so that, no matter what the relationship between parents, their children
played together and shared their food.

One day a neighbour offered a piece of yam to Chike,
who was only four years old. The boy shook his head
haughtily and said, "We don't eat heathen food." The
neighbour was full of rage, but she controlled herself and
only muttered under her breath that even an *Osu* was full
of pride nowadays, thanks to the white man.

And she was right. In the past an *Osu* could not raise
his shaggy head in the presence of the free-born. He was
a slave to one of the many gods of the clan. He was a thing
set apart, not to be venerated but to be despised and almost spat on. He could not marry a free-born, and he
could not take any of the titles of his clan. When he died,
he was buried by his kind in the Bad Bush.

Now all that had changed, or had begun to change. So
that an *Osu* child could even look down his nose at a free-
born, and talk about heathen food! The white man had
indeed accomplished many things.

Chike's father was not originally an *Osu*, but had gone
and married an *Osu* woman in the name of Christianity.
It was unheard of for a man to make himself *Osu* in that
way, with his eyes wide open. But then Amos was nothing
if not mad. The new religion had gone to his head. It was
like palm-wine. Some people drank it and remained sensible. Others lost every sense in their stomach.

The only person who supported Amos in his mad marriage venture was Mr. Brown, the white missionary, who

lived in a thatch-roofed, red-earth-walled parsonage and
was highly respected by the people, not because of his
sermons, but because of a dispensary he ran in one of his
rooms. Amos had emerged from Mr. Brown's parsonage
greatly fortified. A few days later he told his widowed
mother, who had recently been converted to Christianity
and had taken the name Elizabeth. The shock nearly
killed her. When she recovered, she went down on her
knees and begged Amos not to do this thing. But he
would not hear; his ears had been nailed up. At last, in
desperation, Elizabeth went to consult the diviner.

This diviner was a man of great power and wisdom.
As he sat on the floor of his hut beating a tortoise shell,
a coating of white chalk round his eyes, he saw not only
the present, but also what had been and what was to be.
He was called "the man of the four eyes." As soon as old
Elizabeth appeared, he cast his stringed cowries and told
her what she had come to see him about. "Your son has
joined the white man's religion. And you too in your old
age when you should know better. And do you wonder
that he is stricken with insanity? Those who gather ant-
infested faggots must be prepared for the visit of lizards."
He cast his cowries a number of times and wrote with a
finger on a bowl of sand, and all the while his *nwifulu*, a
talking calabash, chatted to itself. "Shut up!" he roared,
and it immediately held its peace. The diviner then muttered a few incantations and rattled off a breathless reel
of proverbs that followed one another like the cowries
in his magic string.

At last he pronounced the cure. The ancestors were
angry and must be appeased with a goat. Old Elizabeth

performed the rites, but her son remained insane and married an *Osu* girl whose name was Sarah. Old Elizabeth renounced her new religion and returned to the faith of her people.

We have wandered from our main story. But it is important to know how Chike's father became an *Osu*, because even today when everything is upside down, such a story is very rare. But now to return to Chike who refused heathen food at the tender age of four years, or may be five.

Two years later he went to the village school. His right hand could now reach across his head to his left ear, which proved that he was old enough to tackle the mysteries of the white man's learning. He was very happy about his new slate and pencil, and especially about his school uniform of white shirt and brown khaki shorts. But as the first day of the new term approached, his young mind dwelt on the many stories about teachers and their canes. And he remembered the song his elder sisters sang, a song that had a somewhat disquieting refrain:

Onye nkuzi ewelu itali piagbusie umuaka.

One of the ways an emphasis is laid in Ibo is by exaggeration, so that the teacher in the refrain might not actually have flogged the children to death. But there was no doubt he did flog them. And Chike thought very much about it.

Being so young, Chike was sent to what was called the "religious class" where they sang, and sometimes danced,

the catechism. He loved the sound of words and he loved
rhythm. During the catechism lesson the class formed a
ring to dance the teacher's question. "Who was Caesar?"
he might ask, and the song would burst forth with much
stamping of feet.

> *Siza bu eze Rome*
> *Onye nachi enu uwa dum.*

It did not matter to their dancing that in the twentieth
century Caesar was no longer ruler of the whole world.

And sometimes they even sang in English. Chike was
very fond of "Ten Green Bottles." They had been taught
the words but they only remembered the first and the
last lines. The middle was hummed and hie-ed and
mumbled:

> *Ten grin botr angin on dar war,*
> *Ten grin botr angin on dar war,*
> *Hm hm hm hm hm*
> *Hm, hm hm hm hm hm,*
> *An ten grin botr angin on dar war.*

In this way the first year passed. Chike was promoted
to the "Infant School," where work of a more serious nature was undertaken.

We need not follow him through the Infant School.
It would make a full story in itself. But it was no differ-
ent from the story of other children. In the Primary
School, however, his individual character began to show.
He developed a strong hatred for arithmetic. But he
loved stories and songs. And he liked particularly the

sound of English words, even when they conveyed no
meaning at all. Some of them simply filled him with ela-
tion. "Periwinkle" was such a word. He had now forgot-
ten how he learned it or exactly what it was. He had a
vague private meaning for it and it was something to do
with fairyland. "Constellation" was another.

Chike's teacher was fond of long words. He was said
to be a very learned man. His favourite pastime was
copying out jaw-breaking words from his *Chambers'
Etymological Dictionary*. Only the other day he had
raised an applause from his class by demolishing a boy's
excuse for lateness with unanswerable erudition. He had
said: "Procrastination is a lazy man's apology." The
teacher's erudition showed itself in every subject he
taught. His nature study lessons were memorable. Chike
would always remember the lesson on the methods of
seed dispersal. According to teacher, there were five
methods: by man, by animals, by water, by wind, and by
explosive mechanism. Even those pupils who forgot all
the other methods remembered "explosive mechanism."

Chike was naturally impressed by teacher's explosive
vocabulary. But the fairyland quality which words had
for him was of a different kind. The first sentences in his
New Method Reader were simple enough and yet they
filled him with a vague exultation: "Once there was a
wizard. He lived in Africa. He went to China to get a
lamp." Chike read it over and over again at home and
then made a song of it. It was a meaningless song. "Peri-
winkles" got into it, and also "Damascus." But it was like
a window through which he saw in the distance a strange,
magical new world. And he was happy.

THE SACRIFICIAL EGG

Julius Obi sat gazing at his typewriter. The fat Chief Clerk, his boss, was snoring at his table. Outside, the gate-keeper in his green uniform was sleeping at his post. You couldn't blame him; no customer had passed through the gate for nearly a week. There was an empty basket on the giant weighing machine. A few palm-kernels lay desolately in the dust around the machine. Only the flies remained in strength.

Julius went to the window that overlooked the great market on the bank of the River Niger. This market, though still called Nkwo, had long spilled over into Eke, Oye, and Afo with the coming of civilization and the growth of the town into a big palm-oil port. In spite of this encroachment, however, it was still busiest on its

original Nkwo day, because the deity who had presided
over it from antiquity still cast her spell only on her own
day—let men in their greed spill over themselves. It was
said that she appeared in the form of an old woman in
the centre of the market just before cock-crow and
waved her magic fan in the four directions of the earth—
in front of her, behind her, to the right and to the left—to
draw to the market men and women from distant places.
And they came bringing the produce of their lands—
palm-oil and kernels, kola nuts, cassava, mats, baskets
and earthenware pots; and took home many-coloured
cloths, smoked fish, iron pots and plates. These were the
forest peoples. The other half of the world who lived by
the great rivers came down also—by canoe, bringing
yams and fish. Sometimes it was a big canoe with a dozen
or more people in it; sometimes it was a lone fisherman
and his wife in a small vessel from the swift-flowing
Anambara. They moored their canoe on the bank and
sold their fish, after much haggling. The woman then
walked up the steep banks of the river to the heart of the
market to buy salt and oil and, if the sales had been very
good, even a length of cloth. And for her children at
home she bought bean cakes and mai-mai which the
Igara women cooked. As evening approached, they took
up their paddles again and paddled away, the water
shimmering in the sunset and their canoe becoming
smaller and smaller in the distance until it was just a dark
crescent on the water's face and two dark bodies swaying
forwards and backwards in it. Umuru then was the meeting place of the forest people who were called Igbo and

the alien riverain folk whom the Igbo called Olu and beyond whom the world stretched in indefiniteness.

Julius Obi was not a native of Umuru. He had come like countless others from some bush village inland. Having passed his Standard Six in a mission school he had come to Umuru to work as a clerk in the offices of the all-powerful European trading company which bought palm-kernels at its own price and sold cloth and metalware, also at its own price. The offices were situated beside the famous market so that in his first two or three weeks Julius had to learn to work within its huge enveloping hum. Sometimes when the Chief Clerk was away he walked to the window and looked down on the vast ant-hill activity. Most of these people were not there yesterday, he thought, and yet the market had been just as full. There must be many, many people in the world to be able to fill the market day after day like this. Of course they say not all who came to the great market were real people. Janet's mother, Ma, had said so.

"Some of the beautiful young women you see squeezing through the crowds are not people like you or me but mammy-wota who have their town in the depths of the river," she said. "You can always tell them, because they are beautiful with a beauty that is too perfect and too cold. You catch a glimpse of her with the tail of your eye, then you blink and look properly, but she has already vanished in the crowd."

Julius thought about these things as he now stood at the window looking down on the silent, empty market. Who would have believed that the great boisterous market could ever be quenched like this? But such was the strength of Kitikpa, the incarnate power of smallpox. Only he could drive away all those people and leave the market to the flies.

When Umuru was a little village, there was an age-grade who swept its market-square every Nkwo day. But progress had turned it into a busy, sprawling, crowded and dirty river port, a no-man's-land where strangers outnumbered by far the sons of the soil, who could do nothing about it except shake their heads at this gross perversion of their prayer. For indeed they had prayed—who will blame them—for their town to grow and prosper. And it had grown. But there is good growth and there is bad growth. The belly does not bulge out only with food and drink; it might be the abominable disease which would end by sending its sufferer out of the house even before he was fully dead.

The strangers who came to Umuru came for trade and money, not in search of duties to perform, for they had those in plenty back home in their village which was real home.

And as if this did not suffice, the young sons and daughters of Umuru soil, encouraged by schools and churches were behaving no better than the strangers. They neglected all their old tasks and kept only the revelries.

Such was the state of the town when Kitikpa came to see it and to demand the sacrifice the inhabitants owed the gods of the soil. He came in confident knowledge of the terror he held over the people. He was an evil deity, and boasted it. Lest he be offended those he killed were not killed but decorated, and no one dared weep for them. He put an end to the coming and going between neighbours and between villages. They said, "Kitikpa is in that village," and immediately it was cut off by its neighbours.

Julius was sad and worried because it was almost a week since he had seen Janet, the girl he was going to marry. Ma had explained to him very gently that he should no longer go to see them "until this thing is over, by the power of Jehovah." (Ma was a very devout Christian convert and one reason why she approved of Julius for her only daughter was that he sang in the choir of the CMS church.)

"You must keep to your rooms," she had said in hushed tones, for Kitikpa strictly forbade any noise or boisterousness. "You never know whom you might meet on the streets. That family has got it." She lowered her voice even more and pointed surreptitiously at the house across the road whose doorway was barred with a yellow palm-frond. "He has decorated one of them already and the rest were moved away today in a big government lorry."

Janet walked a short way with Julius and stopped; so he stopped too. They seemed to have nothing to say to each other yet they lingered on. Then she said goodnight and he said goodnight. And they shook hands, which was very odd, as though parting for the night were something new and grave.

He did not go straight home, because he wanted desperately to cling, even alone, to this strange parting. Being educated he was not afraid of whom he might meet, so he went to the bank of the river and just walked up and down it. He must have been there a long time be-

cause he was still there when the wooden gong of the
night-mask sounded. He immediately set out for home,
half-walking and half-running, for night-masks were not
a matter of superstition; they were real. They chose the
night for their revelry because like the bat's their ugliness
was great.

In his hurry he stepped on something that broke with
a slight liquid explosion. He stopped and peeped down
at the footpath. The moon was not up yet but there was
a faint light in the sky which showed that it would not be
long delayed. In this half-light he saw that he had
stepped on an egg offered in sacrifice. Someone op-
pressed by misfortune had brought the offering to the
crossroads in the dusk. And he had stepped on it. There
were the usual young palm-fronds around it. But Julius
saw it differently as a house where the terrible artist was
at work. He wiped the sole of his foot on the sandy path
and hurried away, carrying another vague worry in his
mind. But hurrying was no use now; the fleet-footed mask
was already abroad. Perhaps it was impelled to hurry by
the threatening imminence of the moon. Its voice rose
high and clear in the still night air like a flaming sword. It
was yet a long way away, but Julius knew that distances
vanished before it. So he made straight for the cocoyam
farm beside the road and threw himself on his belly, in
the shelter of the broad leaves. He had hardly done this
when he heard the rattling staff of the spirit and a thundering stream of esoteric speech. He shook all over. The
sounds came bearing down on him, almost pressing his
face into the moist earth. And now he could hear the foot-
steps. It was as if twenty evil men were running together.

Panic sweat broke all over him and he was nearly impelled to get up and run. Fortunately he kept a firm hold on himself . . . In no time at all the commotion in the air and on the earth—the thunder and torrential rain, the earthquake and flood—passed and disappeared in the distance on the other side of the road.

The next morning, at the office the Chief Clerk, a son of the soil spoke bitterly about last night's provocation of Kitikpa by the headstrong youngsters who had launched the noisy fleet-footed mask in defiance of their elders, who knew that Kitikpa would be enraged, and then . . .

The trouble was that the disobedient youths had never yet experienced the power of Kitikpa themselves; they had only heard of it. But soon they would learn.

As Julius stood at the window looking out on the emptied market he lived through the terror of that night again. It was barely a week ago but already it seemed like another life, separated from the present by a vast emptiness. This emptiness deepened with every passing day. On this side of it stood Julius, and on the other Ma and Janet whom the dread artist decorated.

VENGEFUL CREDITOR

"MADAME, this way," sang the alert, high-wigged sales-girl minding one of a row of cash machines in the super-market. Mrs. Emenike veered her full-stacked trolley ever so lightly to the girl.

"Madame, you were coming to me," complained the cheated girl at the next machine.

"Ah, sorry my dear. Next time."

"Good afternoon, Madame," sang the sweet-voiced girl already unloading Madame's purchases on to her counter.

"Cash or account, Madame?"

"Cash."

She punched the prices as fast as lightning and announced the verdict. Nine pounds fifteen and six. Mrs. Emenike opened her handbag, brought out from it a wallet, unzipped it and held out two clean and crisp five-pound notes. The girl punched again and the machine released a tray of cash. She put Madame's money away and gave her her change and a foot-long receipt. Mrs. Emenike glanced at the bottom of the long strip of paper where the polite machine had registered her total spending with the words THANK YOU COME AGAIN, and nodded.

It was at this point that the first hitch occurred. There seemed to be nobody around to load Madame's purchases into a carton and take them to her car outside.

"Where are these boys?" said the girl almost in distress. "Sorry, Madame. Many of our carriers have gone away because of this free primary . . . John!" she called out, as she caught sight of one of the remaining few, "Come and pack Madame's things!"

John was a limping forty-year-old boy sweating profusely even in the air-conditioned comfort of the supermarket. As he put the things into an empty carton he grumbled aloud.

"I don talk say make una tell Manager make e go fin' more people for dis monkey work."

"You never hear say everybody don go to free primary?" asked the wigged girl, jovially.

"All right-o. But I no go kill myself for sake of free primary."

Out in the car-park he stowed the carton away in the boot of Mrs. Emenike's grey Mercedes and then straightened up to wait while she opened her handbag and then her wallet and stirred a lot of coins there with one finger until she found a three-penny piece, pulled it out between two fingers and dropped it into the carrier's palm.

He hesitated for a while and then limped away without saying a word.

Mrs. Emenike never cared for these old men running little boys' errands. No matter what you gave them they never seemed satisfied. Look at this grumbling cripple. How much did he expect to be given for carrying a tiny carton a few yards? That was what free primary education had brought. It had brought even worse to the homes. Mrs. Emenike had lost three servants including her baby-nurse since the beginning of the school year. The baby-nurse problem was of course the worst. What was a working woman with a seven-month-old baby supposed to do?

However the problem did not last. After only a term of free education the government withdrew the scheme for fear of going bankrupt. It would seem that on the advice of its experts the Education Ministry had planned initially for eight hundred thousand children. In the event one million and a half turned up on the first day of school. Where did all the rest come from? Had the experts misled the government? The chief statistician, interviewed on the radio, said it was nonsense to talk about a miscalculation. The trouble was simply that children from neighbouring states had been brought in in thousands and registered dishonestly by unscrupulous people, a clear case of sabotage.

Whatever the reason the government cancelled the scheme. The *New Age* wrote an editorial praising the Prime Minister for his statesmanship and courage but pointing out that the whole dismal affair could have been avoided if the government had listened in the first place to the warning of many knowledgeable and responsible citizens. Which was true enough, for these citizens had written on the pages of the *New Age* to express their doubt and reservation about free education. The newspaper, on throwing open its pages to a thorough airing of views on the matter, had pointed out that it did so in the national cause and, mounting an old hobby-horse, challenged those of its critics who could see no merit whatever in a newspaper owned by foreign capital to come forward and demonstrate an equal or a higher order of national commitment and patriotism, a challenge that none of those critics took up. The offer of space by the *New Age* was taken up eagerly and in the course of ten days at the rate of two or even three articles a day a large number of responsible citizens—lawyers, doctors, merchants, engineers, salesmen, insurance brokers, university lecturers, etc.—had written in criticism of the scheme. No one was against education for the kids, they said, but free education was premature. Someone said that not even the United States of America in all its wealth and power had introduced it yet, how much less . . .

Mr. Emenike read the various contributions with boyish excitement. "I wish civil servants were free to write to the papers," he told his wife at least on three occasions during those ten days.

"This is not bad, but he should have mentioned that this country has made tremendous strides in education since independence because parents know the value of education and will make any sacrifice to find school fees for their children. We are not a nation of Oliver Twists."

His wife was not really interested in all the argument at that stage, because somehow it all seemed to hang in the air. She had some vague, personal doubts about free education, that was all.

"Have you looked at the paper? Mike has written on this thing," said her husband on another occasion.

"Who is Mike?"

"Mike Ogudu."

"Oh, what does he say?"

"I haven't read it yet . . . Oh yes, you can trust Mike to call a spade a spade. See how he begins: 'Free primary education is tantamount to naked Communism'? That's not quite true but that's Mike all over. He thinks someone might come up to nationalize his shipping line. He is so scared of Communism."

"But who wants Communism here?"

"Nobody. That's what I told him the other evening at the Club. But he is so scared. You know one thing? Too much money is bad-o."

The discussion in the Emenike family remained at this intellectual level until one day their "Small Boy," a very bright lad of twelve helping out the cook and understudying the steward, announced he must go home to see his sick father.

"How did you know your Father was sick?" asked Madame.

"My brodder come tell me."

"When did your brother come?"

"Yesterday for evening-time."

"Why didn't you bring him to see me?"

"I no no say Madame go wan see am."

"Why you no talk since yesterday?" asked Mr. Emenike looking up from his newspaper.

"At first I tink say I no go go home. But today one mind tell me say make you go see-am-o; perhaps e de sick too much. So derefore . . ."

"All right. You can go but make sure you are back by tomorrow afternoon otherwise . . ."

"I must return back by morning-time sef."

He didn't come back. Mrs. Emenike was particularly angry because of the lies. She didn't like being out-witted by servants. Look at that little rat imagining him-self clever. She should have suspected something from the way he had been carrying on of late. Now he had gone with a full month's pay which he should lose in lieu of notice. It went to show that kindness to these people did not pay in the least.

A week later the gardener gave notice. He didn't try to hide anything. His elder brother had sent him a mes-sage to return to their village and register for free educa-tion. Mr. Emenike tried to laugh him out of this ridiculous piece of village ignorance.

"Free primary education is for children. Nobody is go-ing to admit an old man like you. How old are you?"

"I am fifteen years of old, sir."

"You are three," sneered Mrs. Emenike. "Come and suck breast."

"You are not fifteen," said Mr. Emenike. "You are at least twenty and no headmaster will admit you into a primary school. If you want to go and try, by all means do. But don't come back here when you've gone and failed."

"I no go fail, oga," said the gardener. "One man for our village wey old pass my fader sef done register everyting finish. He just go for Magistrate Court and pay dem five shilling and dey swear-am for Court juju wey no de kill porson; e no fit kill rat sef."

"Well it's entirely up to you. Your work here has been good but . . ."

"Mark, what is all that long talk for? He wants to go, let him go."

"Madame, no be say I wan go like dat. But my senior brodder . . ."

"We have heard. You can go now."

"But I no de go today. I wan give one week notice. And I fit find anoder gardener for Madame."

"Don't worry about notice or gardener. Just go away."

"I fit get my pay now or I go come back for afternoon-time?"

"What pay?"

"Madame, for dis ten days I don work for dis mont."

"Don't annoy me any further. Just go away."

But real annoyance was yet to come for Mrs. Emenike. Abigail, the baby-nurse, came up to her two mornings later as she was getting ready for work and dumped the baby in her lap and took off. Abigail of all people! After all she had done for her. Abigail who came to her full of craw-craw, who used rags for sanitary towels, who was so ignorant she gave the baby a full bowl of water to stop it crying and dropped some through its nose. Now Abigail was a lady; she could sew and bake, wear a bra and clean pants, put on powder and perfumes and stretch her hair; and she was ready to go.

From that day Mrs. Emenike hated the words "free primary" which had suddenly become part of everyday language, especially in the villages where they called it "free primadu." She was particularly angry when people made jokes about it and had a strong urge to hit them on the head for a lack of feeling and good taste. And she hated the Americans and the embassies (but particularly the Americans) who threw their money around and enticed the few remaining servants away from Africans. This began when she learnt later that her gardener had not gone to school at all but to a Ford Foundation man who had offered him seven pounds, and bought him a bicycle and a Singer sewing-machine for his wife.

"Why do they do it?" she asked. She didn't really want or need an answer but her husband gave one all the same.

"Because," said he, "back home in America they couldn't possibly afford a servant. So when they come out here and find them so cheap they go crazy. That's why."

Three months later free primary ended and school fees were brought back. The government was persuaded by then that its "piece of hare-brained socialism" as the *New Age* called it was unworkable in African conditions. This was a jibe at the Minister of Education who was notorious for his leftist sympathies and was perpetually at war with the formidable Minister of Finance.

"We cannot go through with this scheme unless we are prepared to impose new taxes," said the Finance Minister at a Cabinet meeting.

"Well then, let's impose the taxes," said the Minister of Education, which provoked derisive laughter from all his colleagues and even from Permanent Secretaries like

Mr. Emenike who were in attendance and who in strict protocol should not participate in debate or laughter.

"We can't," said the Finance Minister indulgently with laughter still in his mouth. "I know my right honourable friend here doesn't worry whether or not this government lasts its full term, but some of us others do. At least I want to be here long enough to retire my election debts . . ."

This was greeted with hilarious laughter and cries of "Hear! Hear!" In debating skill Education was no match for Finance. In fact Finance had no equal in the entire Cabinet, the Prime Minister included.

"Let us make no mistake about it," he continued with a face and tone now serious, "if any one is so foolish as to impose new taxes now on our long-suffering masses . . ."

"I thought we didn't have masses in Africa," interrupted the Minister of Education starting a meagre laughter that was taken up in good sport by one or two others.

"I am sorry to trespass in my right honourable friend's territory; communist slogans are so infectious. But as I was saying we should not talk lightly about new taxes unless we are prepared to bring the Army out to quell tax riots. One simple fact of life which we have come to learn rather painfully and reluctantly—and I'm not so sure even now that we have all learnt it—is that people do riot against taxes but not against school fees. The reason is simple. Everybody, even a motor-park tout, knows what school fees are for. He can see his child going to school in the morning and coming back in the afternoon. But you go and tell him about general taxation and he immediately thinks that government is stealing his money

from him. One other point, if a man doesn't want to pay
school fees he doesn't have to, after all this is a demo-
cratic society. The worst that can happen is that his child
stays at home which he probably doesn't mind at all. But
taxes are different; everybody must pay whether they
want to or not. The difference is pretty sharp. That's why
mobs riot." A few people said "Hear! Hear!" Others just
let out exhalations of relief or agreement. Mr. Emenike
who had an unrestrainable admiration for the Finance
Minister and had been nodding like a lizard through his
speech shouted his "Hear! Hear!" too loud and got a
scorching look from the Prime Minister.

A few desultory speeches followed and the government took its decision not to abolish free primary education but to suspend it until all the relevant factors had
been thoroughly examined.

One little girl of ten, named Veronica, was broken-
hearted. She had come to love school as an escape from
the drabness and arduous demands of home. Her mother,
a near-destitute widow who spent all hours of the day in
the farm and, on market days, in the market left Vero to
carry the burden of caring for the younger children. Actually only the youngest, aged one, needed much looking
after. The other two, aged seven and four, being old
enough to fend for themselves, picking palm-kernels and
catching grasshoppers to eat, were no problem at all to
Vero. But Mary was different. She cried a lot even after
she had been fed her midmorning foo-foo and soup
saved for her (with a little addition of water to the soup)
from breakfast which was itself a diluted left-over from

last night's supper. Mary could not manage palm-kernels on her own account yet so Vero half-chewed them first before passing them on to her. But even after the food and the kernels and grasshoppers and the bowls of water Mary was rarely satisfied, even though her belly would be big and tight like a drum and shine like a mirror.

Their widowed mother, Martha, was a hard-luck woman. She had had an auspicious beginning long, long ago as a pioneer pupil at St. Monica's, then newly founded by white women-missionaries to train the future wives of native evangelists. Most of her schoolmates of those days had married young teachers and were now wives of pastors and one or two even of bishops. But Martha, encouraged by her teacher, Miss Robinson, had married a young carpenter trained by white artisan-missionaries at the Onitsha Industrial Mission, a trade school founded in the fervent belief that if the black man was to be redeemed he needed to learn the Bible along-side manual skills. (Miss Robinson was very keen on the Industrial Mission whose Principal she herself later mar-ried.) But in spite of the bright hopes of those early evangelical days carpentry never developed very much in the way teaching and clerical jobs were to develop. So when Martha's husband died (or as those missionary artisans who taught him long ago might have put it— when he was called to higher service in the heavenly mansions by Him who was Himself once a Carpenter on earth) he left her in complete ruins. It had been a bad-luck marriage from the start. To begin with she had had to wait twenty whole years after their marriage for her first child to be born, so that now she was virtually an old

woman with little children to care for and little strength
left for her task. Not that she was bitter about that. She
was simply too overjoyed that God in His mercy had
lifted her curse of barrenness to feel a need to grumble.
What she nearly did grumble about was the disease that
struck her husband and paralysed his right arm for five
years before his death. It was a trial too heavy and unfair.

Soon after Vero withdrew from school Mr. Mark Emenike, the big government man of their village who lived
in the capital, called on Martha. His Mercedes 220S
pulled up on the side of the main road and he walked
the 500 yards or so of a narrow unmotorable path to the
widow's hut. Martha was perplexed at the visit of such a
great man and as she bustled about for kolanut she kept
wondering. Soon the great man himself in the hurried
style of modern people cleared up the mystery.

"We have been looking for a girl to take care of our
new baby and today someone told me to inquire about
your girl . . ."

At first Martha was reluctant, but when the great man
offered her £5 for the girl's services in the first year—plus
feeding and clothing and other things—she began to
soften.

"Of course it is not money I am concerned about," she
said, "but whether my daughter will be well cared for."

"You don't have to worry about that, Ma. She will be
treated just like one of our own children. My wife is a
Social Welfare Officer and she knows what it means to
care for children. Your daughter will be happy in our
home, I can tell you that. All she will be required to do is
carry the little baby and give it its milk while my wife is
away at the office and the older children at school."

"Vero and her sister Joy were also at school last term," said Martha without knowing why she said it.

"Yes, I know. That thing the government did is bad, very bad. But my belief is that a child who will be somebody will be somebody whether he goes to school or not. It is all written here, in the palm of the hand."

Martha gazed steadily at the floor and then spoke without raising her eyes. "When I married I said to myself: My daughters will do better than I did. I read Standard Three in those days and I said they will all go to College. Now they will not have even the little I had thirty years ago. When I think of it my heart wants to burst."

"Ma, don't let it trouble you too much. As I said before, what anyone of us is going to be is all written here, no matter what the difficulties."

"Yes. I pray God that what is written for these children will be better than what He wrote for me and my husband."

"Amen! . . . And as for this girl if she is obedient and good in my house what stops my wife and me sending her to school when the baby is big enough to go about on his own? Nothing. And she is still a small girl. How old is she?"

"She is ten."

·"You see? She is only a baby. There is plenty of time for her to go to school."

He knew that the part about sending her to school was only a manner of speaking. And Martha knew too. But Vero who had been listening to everything from a dark corner of the adjoining room did not. She actually worked out in her mind the time it would take the baby to go about on his own and it came out quite short. So she went happily to live in the capital in a great man's family and looked after a baby who would soon be big enough to go about on his own and then she would have a chance to go to school.

Vero was a good girl and very sharp. Mr. Emenike and his wife were very pleased with her. She had the sense of a girl twice her age and was amazingly quick to learn.

Mrs. Emenike, who had almost turned sour over her recent difficulty in getting good servants, was now her old self again. She could now laugh about the fiasco of free primadu. She told her friends that now she could go anywhere and stay as long as she liked without worrying about her little man. She was so happy with Vero's work and manners that she affectionately nicknamed her "Little Madame." The nightmare of the months following Abigail's departure was mercifully at an end. She had sought high and low then for another baby-nurse and just couldn't find one. One rather over-ripe young lady had presented herself and asked for seven pounds a month. But it wasn't just the money. It was her general air—a kind of labour-exchange attitude which knew all the rights in the labour code, including presumably the right to have abortions in your servants' quarters and even have a go at your husband. Not that Mark was that way but the girl just wasn't right. After her no other person had turned up until now.

Every morning as the older Emenike children—three girls and a boy—were leaving for school in their father's Mercedes or their mother's little noisy Fiat, Vero would bring the baby out to the steps to say bye-bye. She liked their fine dresses and shoes—she'd never worn any shoes in her life—but what she envied them most was simply the going away every morning, going away from home, from familiar things and tasks. In the first months this envy was very, very mild. It lay beneath the joy of the big going away from the village, from her mother's drab hut, from eating palm-kernels that twisted the intestines at midday, from bitter-leaf soup without fish. That going away was something enormous. But as the months passed the hunger grew for these other little daily departures in fine dresses and shoes and sandwiches and biscuits wrapped in beautiful paper-napkins in dainty little school bags. One morning, as the Fiat took the children away and little Goddy began to cry on Vero's back, a song sprang into her mind to quieten him:

> *Little noisy motor-car*
> *If you're going to the school*
> *Please carry me*
> *Pee—pee—pee!—poh—poh—poh!*

All morning she sang her little song and was pleased with it. When Mr. Emenike dropped the other children home at one o'clock and took off again Vero taught them her new song. They all liked it and for days it supplanted "Baa Baa Black Sheep" and "Simple Simon" and the other songs they brought home from school.

"The girl is a genius," said Mr. Emenike when the new song finally got to him. His wife who heard it first had nearly died from laughter. She had called Vero and said to her, "So you make fun of my car, naughty girl." Vero

was happy because she saw not anger but laughter in
the woman's eyes.

"She is a genius," said her husband. "And she hasn't
been to school."

"And besides she knows you ought to buy me a new
car."

"Never mind, dear. Another year and you can have
that sports car."

"Na so."

"So you don't believe me? Just you wait and see."

More weeks and months passed and little Goddy was
beginning to say a few words but still no one spoke about
Vero's going to school. She decided it was Goddy's fault,
that he wasn't growing fast enough. And he was becoming rather too fond of riding on her back even though he
could walk perfectly well. In fact his favourite words
were "Cayi me." Vero made a song about that too and it
showed her mounting impatience:

> *Carry you! Carry you!*
> *Every time I carry you!*
> *If you no wan grow again*
> *I mus leave you and go school*
> *Because Vero e don tire!*
> *Tire, tire e don tire!*

She sang it all morning until the other children returned from school and then she stopped. She only sang
this one when she was alone with Goddy.

One afternoon Mrs. Emenike returned from work and noticed a redness on Vero's lips.

"Come here," she said, thinking of her expensive lipstick. "What is that?"

It turned out, however, not to be lipstick at all, only her husband's red ink. She couldn't help a smile then.

"And look at her finger-nails! And toes too! So, Little Madame, that's what you do when we go out and leave you at home to mind the baby? You dump him somewhere and begin to paint yourself. Don't ever let me catch you with that kind of nonsense again; do you hear?" It occurred to her to strengthen her warning somehow if only to neutralize the smile she had smiled at the beginning.

"Do you know that red ink is poisonous? You want to kill yourself. Well, little lady you have to wait till you leave my house and return to your mother."

That did it, she thought in glowing self-satisfaction. She could see that Vero was suitably frightened. Throughout the rest of that afternoon she walked about like a shadow.

When Mr. Emenike came home she told him the story as he ate a late lunch. And she called Vero for him to see.

"Show him your finger-nails," she said. "And your toes, Little Madame!"

"I see," he said waving Vero away. "She is learning fast. Do you know the proverb which says that when mother-cow chews giant grass her little calves watch her mouth?"

"Who is a cow? You rhinoceros!"

"It is only a proverb, my dear."

A week or so later Mrs. Emenike just home from work noticed that the dress she had put on the baby in the morning had been changed into something much too warm.

"What happened to the dress I put on him?"

"He fell down and soiled it. So I changed him," said Vero. But there was something very strange in her manner. Mrs. Emenike's first thought was that the child must have had a bad fall.

"Where did he fall?" she asked in alarm. "Where did he hit on the ground? Bring him to me! What is all this? Blood? No? What is it? My God has killed me! Go and bring me the dress. At once!"

"I washed it," said Vero beginning to cry, a thing she had never done before. Mrs. Emenike rushed out to the line and brought down the blue dress and the white vest both heavily stained red!

She seized Vero and beat her in a mad frenzy with both hands. Then she got a whip and broke it all on her until her face and arms ran with blood. Only then did Vero admit making the child drink a bottle of red ink. Mrs. Emenike collapsed into a chair and began to cry.

Mr. Emenike did not wait to have lunch. They bundled Vero into the Mercedes and drove her the forty miles to her mother in the village. He had wanted to go alone but his wife insisted on coming, and taking the baby too. He stopped on the main road as usual. But he didn't go in with the girl. He just opened the door of the car, pulled her out and his wife threw her little bundle of clothes after her. And they drove away again.

Martha returned from the farm tired and grimy. Her children rushed out to meet her and to tell her that Vero was back and was crying in their bedroom. She practically dropped her basket and went to see; but she couldn't make any sense of her story.

"You gave the baby red ink? Why? So that you can go to school? How? Come on. Let's go to their place. Perhaps they will stay in the village overnight. Or else they will have told somebody there what happened. I don't understand your story. Perhaps you stole something. Not so?"

"Please Mama don't take me back there. They will kill me."

"Come on, since you won't tell me what you did."

She seized her wrist and dragged her outside. Then in the open she saw all the congealed blood on whip-marks all over her head, face, neck and arms. She swallowed hard.

"Who did this?"

"My Madame."

"And what did you say you did? You must tell me."

"I gave the baby red ink."

"All right, then let's go."

Vero began to wail louder. Martha seized her by the wrist again and they set off. She neither changed her work clothes nor even washed her face and hands. Every woman—and sometimes the men too—they passed on the way screamed on seeing Vero's whip-marks and wanted to know who did it. Martha's reply to all was "I don't know yet. I am going to find out."

She was lucky. Mr. Emenike's big car was there, so they had not returned to the capital. She knocked at their front door and walked in. Mrs. Emenike was sitting there

in the parlour giving bottled food to the baby but she ig-
nored the visitors completely neither saying a word to
them nor even looking in their direction. It was her husband who descended the stairs a little later who told the
story. As soon as the meaning dawned on Martha—that
the red ink was given to the baby *to drink* and that the
motive was to encompass its death—she screamed, with
two fingers plugging her ears, that she wanted to hear no
more. At the same time she rushed outside, tore a twig off
a flowering shrub and by clamping her thumb and fore-
finger at one end and running them firmly along its full
length stripped it of its leaves in one quick movement.
Armed with the whip she rushed back to the house crying
"I have heard an abomination!" Vero was now screaming
and running round the room.

"Don't touch her here in my house," said Mrs. Emenike,
cold and stern as an oracle, noticing her visitors for the
first time. "Take her away from here at once. You want
to show me your shock. Well I don't want to see. Go and
show your anger in your own house. Your daughter did
not learn murder here in my house."

This stung Martha deep in her spirit and froze her in
mid-stride. She stood rooted to the spot, her whip-hand
lifeless by her side. "My Daughter," she said finally ad-
dressing the younger woman, "as you see me here I am
poor and wretched but I am not a murderer. If my
daughter Vero is to become a murderer God knows she
cannot say she learnt from me."

"Perhaps it's from me she learnt," said Mrs. Emenike
showing her faultless teeth in a terrible false smile, "or
maybe she snatched it from the air. That's right, she

snatched it from the air. Look, woman, take your daughter and leave my house."

"Vero, let's go; come, let's go!"

"Yes, please go!"

Mr. Emenike who had been trying vainly to find an opening for the clearly needed male intervention now spoke.

"It is the work of the devil," he said. "I have always known that the craze for education in this country will one day ruin all of us. Now even children will commit murder in order to go to school."

This clumsy effort to mollify all sides at once stung Martha even more. As she jerked Vero homewards by the hand she clutched her unused whip in her other hand. At first she rained abuses on the girl, called her an evil child that entered her mother's womb by the back of the house.

"Oh God, what have I done?" Her tears began to flow now. "If I had had a child with other women of my age, that girl that calls me murderer might have been no older than my daughter. And now she spits in my face. That's what you brought me to," she said to the crown of Vero's head, and jerked her along more violently.

"I will kill you today. Let's get home first."

Then a strange revolt, vague, undirected began to well up at first slowly inside her. "And that thing that calls himself a man talks to me about the craze for education. All his children go to school, even the one that is only two years; but that is no craze. Rich people have no craze. It is only when the children of poor widows like me want to go with the rest that it becomes a craze. What is this life? To God, what is it? And now my child thinks she must kill the baby she is hired to tend before she can get a chance. Who put such an abomination into her belly? God, you know I did not."

She threw away the whip and with her freed hand wiped her tears.

DEAD MEN'S PATH

MICHAEL OBI's hopes were fulfilled much earlier than he had expected. He was appointed headmaster of Ndume Central School in January 1949. It had always been an unprogressive school, so the Mission authorities decided to send a young and energetic man to run it. Obi accepted this responsibility with enthusiasm. He had many wonderful ideas and this was an opportunity to put them into practice. He had had sound secondary school education which designated him a "pivotal teacher" in the official records and set him apart from the other headmasters in the mission field. He was outspoken in his condemnation of the narrow views of these older and often less-educated ones.

"We shall make a good job of it, shan't we?" he asked

his young wife when they first heard the joyful news of
his promotion.

"We shall do our best," she replied. "We shall have such
beautiful gardens and everything will be just *modern*
and delightful . . ." In their two years of married life she
had become completely infected by his passion for
"modern methods" and his denigration of "these old and
superannuated people in the teaching field who would be
better employed as traders in the Onitsha market." She
began to see herself already as the admired wife of the
young headmaster, the queen of the school.

The wives of the other teachers would envy her posi-
tion. She would set the fashion in everything . . . Then,
suddenly, it occurred to her that there might not be other
wives. Wavering between hope and fear, she asked her
husband, looking anxiously at him.

"All our colleagues are young and unmarried," he said
with enthusiasm which for once she did not share. "Which
is a good thing," he continued.

"Why?"

"Why? They will give all their time and energy to the
school."

Nancy was downcast. For a few minutes she became
sceptical about the new school; but it was only for a few
minutes. Her little personal misfortune could not blind
her to her husband's happy prospects. She looked at him
as he sat folded up in a chair. He was stoop-shouldered
and looked frail. But he sometimes surprised people with
sudden bursts of physical energy. In his present posture,
however, all his bodily strength seemed to have retired
behind his deep-set eyes, giving them an extraordinary

power of penetration. He was only twenty-six, but looked thirty or more. On the whole, he was not unhandsome.

"A penny for your thoughts, Mike," said Nancy after a while, imitating the woman's magazine she read.

"I was thinking what a grand opportunity we've got at last to show these people how a school should be run."

Ndume School was backward in every sense of the word. Mr. Obi put his whole life into the work, and his wife hers too. He had two aims. A high standard of teaching was insisted upon, and the school compound was to be turned into a place of beauty. Nancy's dream-gardens came to life with the coming of the rains, and blossomed. Beautiful hibiscus and allamanda hedges in brilliant red and yellow marked out the carefully tended school compound from the rank neighbourhood bushes.

One evening as Obi was admiring his work he was scandalized to see an old woman from the village hobble right across the compound, through a marigold flower-bed and the hedges. On going up there he found faint signs of an almost disused path from the village across the school compound to the bush on the other side.

"It amazes me," said Obi to one of his teachers who had been three years in the school, "that you people allowed the villagers to make use of this footpath. It is simply incredible." He shook his head.

"The path," said the teacher apologetically, "appears to be very important to them. Although it is hardly used, it connects the village shrine with their place of burial."

"And what has that got to do with the school?" asked the headmaster.

"Well, I don't know," replied the other with a shrug of the shoulders. "But I remember there was a big row some time ago when we attempted to close it."

"That was some time ago. But it will not be used now," said Obi as he walked away. "What will the Government Education Officer think of this when he comes to inspect the school next week? The villagers might, for all I know, decide to use the schoolroom for a pagan ritual during the inspection."

Heavy sticks were planted closely across the path at the two places where it entered and left the school premises. These were further strengthened with barbed wire.

Three days later the village priest of *Ani* called on the headmaster. He was an old man and walked with a slight stoop. He carried a stout walking-stick which he usually tapped on the floor, by way of emphasis, each time he made a new point in his argument.

"I have heard," he said after the usual exchange of cordialities, "that our ancestral footpath has recently been closed . . ."

"Yes," replied Mr. Obi. "We cannot allow people to make a highway of our school compound."

"Look here, my son," said the priest bringing down his walking-stick, "this path was here before you were born and before your father was born. The whole life of this village depends on it. Our dead relatives depart by it and our ancestors visit us by it. But most important, it is the path of children coming in to be born . . ."

Mr. Obi listened with a satisfied smile on his face.

"The whole purpose of our school," he said finally, "is

to eradicate just such beliefs as that. Dead men do not require footpaths. The whole idea is just fantastic. Our duty is to teach your children to laugh at such ideas."

"What you say may be true," replied the priest, "but we follow the practices of our fathers. If you re-open the path we shall have nothing to quarrel about. What I always say is: let the hawk perch and let the eagle perch." He rose to go.

"I am sorry," said the young headmaster. "But the school compound cannot be a thoroughfare. It is against our regulations. I would suggest your constructing another path, skirting our premises. We can even get our boys to help in building it. I don't suppose the ancestors will find the little detour too burdensome."

"I have no more words to say," said the old priest, already outside.

Two days later a young woman in the village died in childbed. A diviner was immediately consulted and he prescribed heavy sacrifices to propitiate ancestors insulted by the fence.

Obi woke up next morning among the ruins of his work. The beautiful hedges were torn up not just near the path but right round the school, the flowers trampled to death and one of the school buildings pulled down . . . That day, the white Supervisor came to inspect the school and wrote a nasty report on the state of the premises but more seriously about the "tribal-war situation developing between the school and the village, arising in part from the misguided zeal of the new headmaster."

UNCLE BEN'S CHOICE

IN THE YEAR nineteen hundred and nineteen I was a young clerk in the Niger Company at Umuru. To be a clerk in those days is like to be a minister today. My salary was two pounds ten. You may laugh but two pounds ten in those days is like fifty pounds today. You could buy a big goat with four shillings. I could remember the most senior African in the company was one Saro man on ten-thirteen-four. He was like Governor-General in our eyes.

Like all progressive young men I joined the African Club. We played tennis and billiards. Every year we played a tournament with the European Club. But I was less concerned with that. What I liked was the Saturday night dances. Women were surplus. Not all the waw-waw

women you see in townships today but beautiful things
like this.

I had a Raleigh bicycle, brand new, and everybody
called me Jolly Ben. I was selling like hot bread. But there
is one thing about me—we can laugh and joke and drink
and do otherwise but I must always keep my sense with
me. My father told me that a true son of our land must
know how to sleep and keep one eye open. I never forget
it. So I played and laughed with everyone and they
shouted "Jolly Ben! Jolly Ben!" but I knew what I was doing. The women of Umuru are very sharp; before you
count A they count B. So I had to be very careful. I never
showed any of them the road to my house and I never ate
the food they cooked for fear of love medicines. I had
seen many young men kill themselves with women in
those days, so I remembered my father's word: Never let
a handshake pass the elbow.

I can say that the only exception was one tall, yellow,
salt-water girl like this called Margaret. One Sunday
morning I was playing my gramophone, a brand-new
HMV Senior. (I never believe in second-hand things.
If I have no money for a new one I just keep myself quiet;
that is my motto.) I was playing this record and standing
at the window with my chewing-stick in my mouth. People were passing in their fine-fine dresses to one church
nearby. This Margaret was going with them when she
saw me. As luck would have it I did not see her in time
to hide. So that very day—she did not wait till tomorrow
or next tomorrow—but as soon as church closed she returned back. According to her she wanted to convert me
to Roman Catholic. Wonders will never end! Margaret

Jumbo! Beautiful thing like this. But it is not Margaret I want to tell you about now. I want to tell you how I stopped all that foolishness.

It was one New Year's Eve like this. You know how New Year can pass Christmas for jollity, for we end-of-month people. By Christmas Day the month has reached twenty-hungry but on New Year your pocket is heavy. So that day I went to the Club.

When I see you young men of nowadays say you drink, I just laugh. You don't know what drink is. You drink one bottle of beer or one shot of whisky and you begin to holler like craze-man. That night I was taking it easy on White Horse. *All that are desirous to pass from Edinburgh to London or any other place on their road, let them repair to the White Horse cellar. . . .* God Almighty!

One thing with me is I never mix my drinks. The day I want to drink whisky I know that that is whisky-day; if I want to drink beer tomorrow then I know it is beerday; I don't touch any other thing. That night I was on White Horse. I had one roasted chicken and a tin of Guinea Gold. Yes, I used to smoke in those days. I only stopped when one German doctor told me my heart was as black as a cooking-pot. Those German doctors were spirits. You know they used to give injections in the head or belly or anywhere. You just point where the thing is paining you and they give it to you right there—they don't waste time.

What was I saying? . . . Yes, I drank a bottle of White Horse and put one roasted chicken on top of it . . . Drunk? It is not in my dictionary. I have never been drunk in my life. My father used to say that the cure for

drink is to say no. When I want to drink I drink, when I
want to stop I stop. So about three o'clock that night I
said to myself, you have had enough. So I jumped on my
new Raleigh bicycle and went home quietly to sleep.

At that time our senior clerk was jailed for stealing
bales of calico and I was acting in that capacity. So I
lived in a small company house. You know where G. B.
Olivant is today? . . . Yes, overlooking the River Niger.
That is where my house was. I had two rooms on one
side of it and the store-keeper had two rooms on the
other side. But as luck would have it this man was on
leave, so his side was vacant.

I opened the front door and went inside. Then I locked
it again. I left my bicycle in the first room and went into
the bedroom. I was too tired to begin to look for my
lamp. So I pulled my dress and packed them on the back
of the chair, and fell like a log into my big iron bed.
And to God who made me, there was a woman in my
bed. My mind told me at once it was Margaret. So I began to laugh and touch her here and there. She was hundred per cent naked. I continued laughing and asked her
when did she come. She did not say anything and I suspected she was annoyed because she asked me to take
her to the Club that day and I said no. I said to her: if
you come there we will meet, I don't take anybody to
the Club as such. So I suspected that is what is making
her vex.

I told her not to vex but still she did not say anything.
I asked her if she was asleep—just for asking sake. She
said nothing. Although I told you that I did not like
women to come to my house, but for every rule there
must be an exception. So if I say that I was very angry

to find Margaret that night I will be telling a white lie.
I was still laughing when I noticed that her breasts were
straight like the breasts of a girl of sixteen—or seventeen,
at most. I thought that perhaps it was because of the
way she was lying on her back. But when I touched the
hair and it was soft like the hair of a European my laughter was quenched by force. I touched the hair on her
head and it was the same. I jumped out of the bed and
shouted: "Who are you?" My head swelled up like a bar-
rel and I was shaking. The woman sat up and stretched
her hands to call me back; as she did so her fingers
touched me. I jumped back at the same time and
shouted again to her to call her name. Then I said to
myself: How can you be afraid of a woman? Whether
a white woman or a black woman, it is the same ten and
ten pence. So I said: "All right, I will soon open your
mouth," at the same time I began to look for matches on
the table. The woman suspected what I was looking for.
She said, "Biko akpakwana ọku."

I said: "So you are not a white woman. Who are you?
I will strike the matches now if you don't tell me." I
shook the matches to show her that I meant business.
My boldness had come back and I was trying to remember the voice because it was very familiar.

"Come back to the bed and I will tell you," was what
I heard next. Whoever told me it was a familiar voice
told me a lie. It was sweet like sugar but not familiar
at all. So I struck the matches.

"I beg you," was the last thing she said.

If I tell you what I did next or how I managed to come
out of that room it is pure guess-work. The next thing

I remember is that I was running like a craze-man to Matthew's house. Then I was banging on his door with my both hands.

"Who is that?" he said from inside.

"Open," I shouted. "In the name of God above, open."

I called my name but my voice was not like my voice. The door opened very small and I saw my kinsman holding a matchet in his right hand.

I fell down on the floor, and he said, "God will not agree."

It was God Himself who directed me to Matthew Obi's house that night because I did not see where I was going. I could not say whether I was still in this world or whether I was dead. Matthew poured cold water on me and after some time I was able to tell him what happened. I think I told it upside down otherwise he would not keep asking me what was she like, what was she like.

"I told you before I did not see her," I said.

"I see, but you heard her voice?"

"I heard her voice quite all right. And I touched her and she touched me."

"I don't know whether you did well or not to scare her away," was what Matthew said.

I don't know how to explain it but those words from Matthew opened my eyes. I knew at once that I had been visited by Mami Wota, the Lady of the River Niger.

Matthew said again: "It depends what you want in life. If it is wealth you want then you made a great mistake today, but if you are a true son of your father then take my hand."

We shook hands and he said: "Our fathers never told

us that a man should prefer wealth instead of wives and children."

Today whenever my wives make me vex I tell them: "I don't blame you. If I had been wise I would have taken Mami Wota." They laugh and ask me why did I not take her. The youngest one says: "Don't worry, Papa, she will come again; she will come tomorrow." And they laugh again.

But we all know it is a joke. For where is the man who will choose wealth instead of children? Except a crazy white man like Dr. J. M. Stuart-Young. Oh, I didn't tell you. The same night that I drove Mami Wota out she went to Dr. J. M. Stuart-Young, a white merchant and became his lover. You have heard of him? . . . Oh yes, he became the richest man in the whole country. But she did not allow him to marry. When he died, what happened? All his wealth went to outsiders. Is that good wealth? I ask you. God forbid.

CIVIL PEACE

JONATHAN IWEGBU counted himself extra-ordinarily lucky. "Happy survival!" meant so much more to him than just a current fashion of greeting old friends in the first hazy days of peace. It went deep to his heart. He had come out of the war with five inestimable blessings—his head, his wife Maria's head and the heads of three out of their four children. As a bonus he also had his old bicycle—a miracle too but naturally not to be compared to the safety of five human heads.

The bicycle had a little history of its own. One day at the height of the war it was commandeered "for urgent military action." Hard as its loss would have been to him he would still have let it go without a thought had he not had some doubts about the genuineness of the officer.

It wasn't his disreputable rags, nor the toes peeping out
of one blue and one brown canvas shoes, nor yet the two
stars of his rank done obviously in a hurry in biro, that
troubled Jonathan; many good and heroic soldiers looked
the same or worse. It was rather a certain lack of grip
and firmness in his manner. So Jonathan, suspecting he
might be amenable to influence, rummaged in his raffia
bag and produced the two pounds with which he had
been going to buy firewood which his wife, Maria, re-
tailed to camp officials for extra stock-fish and corn meal,
and got his bicycle back. That night he buried it in the
little clearing in the bush where the dead of the camp,
including his own youngest son, were buried. When he
dug it up again a year later after the surrender all it
needed was a little palm-oil greasing. "Nothing puzzles
God," he said in wonder.

He put it to immediate use as a taxi and accumulated
a small pile of Biafran money ferrying camp officials
and their families across the four-mile stretch to the near-
est tarred road. His standard charge per trip was six
pounds and those who had the money were only glad
to be rid of some of it in this way. At the end of a fortnight he had made a small fortune of one hundred and
fifteen pounds.

Then he made the journey to Enugu and found another miracle waiting for him. It was unbelievable. He
rubbed his eyes and looked again and it was still standing there before him. But, needless to say, even that
monumental blessing must be accounted also totally in-
ferior to the five heads in the family. This newest miracle
was his little house in Ogui Overside. Indeed nothing

puzzles God! Only two houses away a huge concrete edifice some wealthy contractor had put up just before the war was a mountain of rubble. And here was Jonathan's little zinc house of no regrets built with mud blocks quite intact! Of course the doors and windows were missing and five sheets off the roof. But what was that? And anyhow he had returned to Enugu early enough to pick up bits of old zinc and wood and soggy sheets of cardboard lying around the neighbourhood before thousands more came out of their forest holes looking for the same things. He got a destitute carpenter with one old hammer, a blunt plane and a few bent and rusty nails in his tool bag to turn this assortment of wood, paper and metal into door and window shutters for five Nigerian shillings or fifty Biafran pounds. He paid the pounds, and moved in with his overjoyed family carrying five heads on their shoulders.

His children picked mangoes near the military cemetery and sold them to soldiers' wives for a few pennies— real pennies this time—and his wife started making breakfast akara balls for neighbours in a hurry to start life again. With his family earnings he took his bicycle to the villages around and bought fresh palm-wine which he mixed generously in his rooms with the water which had recently started running again in the public tap down the road, and opened up a bar for soldiers and other lucky people with good money.

At first he went daily, then every other day and finally once a week, to the offices of the Coal Corporation where he used to be a miner, to find out what was what. The only thing he did find out in the end was that that little

house of his was even a greater blessing than he had
thought. Some of his fellow ex-miners who had nowhere
to return at the end of the day's waiting just slept outside
the doors of the offices and cooked what meal they could
scrounge together in Bournvita tins. As the weeks length-
ened and still nobody could say what was what Jonathan
discontinued his weekly visits altogether and faced his
palm-wine bar.

But nothing puzzles God. Came the day of the wind-
fall when after five days of endless scuffles in queues
and counter-queues in the sun outside the Treasury he
had twenty pounds counted into his palms as ex-gratia
award for the rebel money he had turned in. It was like
Christmas for him and for many others like him when
the payments began. They called it (since few could
manage its proper official name) *egg-rasher*.

As soon as the pound notes were placed in his palm
Jonathan simply closed it tight over them and buried
fist and money inside his trouser pocket. He had to be
extra careful because he had seen a man a couple of
days earlier collapse into near-madness in an instant before that oceanic crowd because no sooner had he got
his twenty pounds than some heartless ruffian picked it
off him. Though it was not right that a man in such an
extremity of agony should be blamed yet many in the
queues that day were able to remark quietly on the vic-
tim's carelessness, especially after he pulled out the in-
nards of his pocket and revealed a hole in it big enough
to pass a thief's head. But of course he had insisted that
the money had been in the other pocket, pulling it out

too to show its comparative wholeness. So one had to be careful.

Jonathan soon transferred the money to his left hand and pocket so as to leave his right free for shaking hands should the need arise, though by fixing his gaze at such an elevation as to miss all approaching human faces he made sure that the need did not arise, until he got home.

He was normally a heavy sleeper but that night he heard all the neighbourhood noises die down one after another. Even the night watchman who knocked the hour on some metal somewhere in the distance had fallen silent after knocking one o'clock. That must have been the last thought in Jonathan's mind before he was finally carried away himself. He couldn't have been gone for long, though, when he was violently awakened again.

"Who is knocking?" whispered his wife lying beside him on the floor.

"I don't know," he whispered back breathlessly.

The second time the knocking came it was so loud and imperious that the rickety old door could have fallen down.

"Who is knocking?" he asked then, his voice parched and trembling.

"Na tief-man and him people," came the cool reply. "Make you hopen de door." This was followed by the heaviest knocking of all.

Maria was the first to raise the alarm, then he followed and all their children.

"Police-o! Thieves-o! Neighbours-o! Police-o! We are lost! We are dead! Neighbours, are you asleep? Wake up! Police-o!"

This went on for a long time and then stopped suddenly. Perhaps they had scared the thief away. There was total silence. But only for a short while.

"You done finish?" asked the voice outside. "Make we help you small. Oya, everybody!"

"Police-o! Tief-man-o! Neighbours-o! we done loss-o! Police-o! . . ."

There were at least five other voices besides the leader's.

Jonathan and his family were now completely paralysed by terror. Maria and the children sobbed inaudibly like lost souls. Jonathan groaned continuously.

The silence that followed the thieves' alarm vibrated horribly. Jonathan all but begged their leader to speak again and be done with it.

"My frien," said he at long last, "we don try our best for call dem but I tink say dem all done sleep-o. . . So wetin we go do now? Sometaim you wan call soja? Or you wan make we call dem for you? Soja better pass police. No be so?"

"Na so!" replied his men. Jonathan thought he heard even more voices now than before and groaned heavily. His legs were sagging under him and his throat felt like sand-paper.

"My frien, why you no de talk again. I de ask you say you wan make we call soja?"

"No."

"Awrighto. Now make we talk business. We no be bad tief. We no like for make trouble. Trouble done finish. War done finish and all the katakata wey de for inside.

No Civil War again. This time na Civil Peace. No be so?"

"Na so!" answered the horrible chorus.

"What do you want from me? I am a poor man. Everything I had went with this war. Why do you come to me? You know people who have money. We . . ."

"Awright! We know say you no get plenty money. But we sef no get even anini. So derefore make you open dis window and give us one hundred pound and we go commot. Orderwise we de come for inside now to show you guitar-boy like dis . . ."

A volley of automatic fire rang through the sky. Maria and the children began to weep aloud again.

"Ah, missisi de cry again. No need for dat. We done talk say we na good tief. We just take our small money and go nwayorly. No molest. Abi we de molest?"

"At all!" sang the chorus.

"My friends," began Jonathan hoarsely. "I hear what you say and I thank you. If I had one hundred pounds . . ."

"Lookia my frien, no be play we come play for your house. If we make mistake and step for inside you no go like am-o. So derefore . . ."

"To God who made me; if you come inside and find one hundred pounds, take it and shoot me and shoot my wife and children. I swear to God. The only money I have in this life is this twenty-pounds *egg-rasher* they gave me today . . ."

"OK. Time de go. Make you open dis window and bring the twenty pound. We go manage am like dat."

There were now loud murmurs of dissent among the chorus: "Na lie de man de lie; e get plenty money . . .

Make we go inside and search properly well . . . Wetin
be twenty pound? . . ."

"Shurrup!" rang the leader's voice like a lone shot in
the sky and silenced the murmuring at once. "Are you
dere? Bring the money quick!"

"I am coming," said Jonathan fumbling in the darkness
with the key of the small wooden box he kept by his side
on the mat.

At the first sign of light as neighbours and others assembled to commiserate with him he was already strap-
ping his five-gallon demijohn to his bicycle carrier and
his wife, sweating in the open fire, was turning over akara
balls in a wide clay bowl of boiling oil. In the corner his
eldest son was rinsing out dregs of yesterday's palm wine
from old beer bottles.

"I count it as nothing," he told his sympathizers, his
eyes on the rope he was tying. "What is *egg-rasher?* Did
I depend on it last week? Or is it greater than other things
that went with the war? I say, let *egg-rasher* perish in the
flames! Let it go where everything else has gone. Nothing
puzzles God."

SUGAR BABY

I CAUGHT the fierce expression on his face in the brief impulsive moment of that strange act; and I understood. I don't mean the symbolism such as it was; that, to me, was pretty superficial and obvious. No. It was rather his deadly earnestness.

It lasted no more than a second or two. Just as long as it took to thrust his hand into his sugar bowl, grasp a handful and fling it out of the window, his squarish jaw set viciously. Then it crumbled again in the gentle solvent of a vague smile.

"Ah-ah; why?" asked one of the other two present, or perhaps both, taken aback and completely mystified.

"Only to show sugar that today I am greater than he, that the day has arrived when I can afford sugar and, if it pleases me, throw sugar away."

They roared with laughter then. Cletus joined them but laughing only moderately. Then I joined too, meagrely.

"You are a funny one, Cletus," said Umera, his huge trunk shaking with mirth and his eyes glistening.

Soon we were drinking Cletus's tea and munching chunks of bread smeared thickly with margarine.

"Yes," said Umera's friend whose name I didn't catch, "may bullet crack sugar's head!"

"Amen."

"One day soon it will be butter's turn," said Umera. "Please excuse my bad habit." He had soaked a wedge of bread in his tea and carried it dripping into his enormous mouth, his head thrown back. "That's how I learnt to eat bread," he contrived out of a full, soggy mouth. He tore another piece—quite small this time—and threw it out of the window. "Go and meet sugar, and bullet crack both your heads!"

"Amen."

"Tell them about me and sugar, Mike, tell them," said Cletus to me.

Well, I said, there was nothing really to tell except that my friend Cletus had what our English friends would call a sweet tooth. But of course the English, a very moderate race, couldn't possibly have a name for anything like Cletus and his complete denture of thirty-two sweet teeth.

It was an old joke of mine but Umera and his friend didn't know it and so graced it with more uproarious laughter. Which was good because I didn't want to tell any of the real stories Cletus was urging. And fortunately

too Umera and his friend were bursting to tell more and
more of their own hardship stories; for most of us had
become in those days like a bunch of old hypochondriac
women vying to recount the most lurid details of their
own special infirmities.

And I found it all painfully, unbearably, pathetic. I
never possessed some people's ability (Cletus's, for ex-
ample) to turn everything to good account. Pain lasts
far longer on me than on him even when—strange to
say—it is his own pain. It wouldn't have occurred to me,
not in a thousand years, to enact that farcical celebration
of victory over sugar. Simply watching it I felt bad. It
was like a man standing you a drink because some fellow
who once seduced his wife had just died, according to
the morning's papers. The drink would stick in my throat
because my pity and my contempt would fall on the
celebrator and my admiration on the gallant man who
once so justly cuckolded him.

For Cletus sugar is not simply sugar. It is what makes
life bearable. We lived and worked together in the last
eighteen months of the war and so I was pretty close to
his agony, to his many humiliating defeats. I never could
understand nor fully sympathise with his addiction. As
long as I had my one gari meal in the afternoon I neither
asked for breakfast nor dinner. At first I had suffered
from the lack of meat or fish and worst of all of salt in
the soup, but by the second year of the war I was noticing
it less and less. But Cletus got more obsessively hinged
to his sugar and tea every single day of deprivation, a
dangerous case of an appetite growing on what it did
not feed on. How he acquired such an alien taste in the

first place I have not even bothered to investigate; it probably began like a lone cancer cell in lonely winter days and nights in the black belt of Ladbroke Grove.

Other tea and coffee drinkers, if they still found any to drink at all, had learnt long ago to take it black and bitter. Then some unrecognized genius had lightened their burden further with the discovery that the blackest coffee taken along with a piece of coconut lost a good deal of its bitter edge. And so a new, sustaining *petit déjeuner* was born. But Cletus like a doomed man must have the proper thing or else nothing at all. Did I say I lost patience with him? Well, sometimes. In more charitable and more thoughtful moments I felt sorrow for him rather than anger, for could one honestly say that an addiction to sugar was any more irrational than all the other many addictions going at the time? No. And it constituted no threat to anybody else, which you couldn't say for all those others.

One day he came home in very high spirits. Some one recently returned from abroad had sold him two dozen tablets of an artificial sweetener for three pounds. He went straight to the kitchen to boil water. Then he brought out from some secure corner of his bag his old tin of instant coffee—he no longer had tea—which had now gone solid. "Nothing wrong with it," he assured me again and again though I hadn't even said a word. "It's the humidity; the smell is quite unimpaired." He sniffed it and then broke off two small rocklike pieces with a knife and made two cups of coffee. Then he sat back with a song in his face.

I could barely stand the taste of the sweetener. It

larded every sip with a lingering cloyingness and
siphoned unsuspected wells of saliva into my mouth. We
drank in silence. Then suddenly Cletus jumped up and
rushed outside to give way to a rasping paroxysm of
vomiting. I stopped then trying to drink what was left
in my cup.

I told him sorry when he came back in. He didn't say
a word. He went straight to his room and fetched a cup
of water and went out again to rinse his mouth. After a
few gargles he tipped the remaining water into a cupped
hand and washed down his face. I said sorry again and
he nodded.

Later he came where I sat. "Do you care for these?"
He held out the little tablets with palpable disgust.
Strange how even one attack of vomiting could so ut-
terly reduce a man. "No, not really. But keep them. I'm
sure we won't need to go far to find friends who do."

He either was not listening or else he simply could not
bring himself to live with the things another minute. He
made his third trip outside and threw them into the same
wild plot of weeds which had just received his vomit.

He must have worked himself to such a pitch of ex-
pectation over the wretched sugar substitute that he now
plummeted headlong into near nervous collapse. For
the next two days he kept to his bed, neither showing
up in the morning at the Directorate where we worked
nor going in the evening as was his custom to see his
girl friend, Mercy.

On the third day I really lost patience with him and
told him a few harsh things about fighting a war of survival, calling to my aid more or less the rhetoric for

which his radio scripts were famous. "Fuck your war!
Fuck your survival!" he shouted at me. All the same he
got better soon afterwards and suitably shamefaced.
Then I relented somewhat myself and began privately
to make serious inquiries about sugar on his behalf.

Another friend at the Directorate told me about a
certain Father Doherty who lived ten miles away and
controlled Caritas relief stores for the entire district. A
well-known and knowing Roman Catholic, my friend, he
warned me that Father Doherty, though a good and
generous man, was apt to be somewhat unpredictable
and had become particularly so lately since a shrapnel
hit him in the head at the airport.

Cletus and I made the journey on the following Saturday and found Father Doherty in reasonably good
mood for a man who had just spent six nights running at
the airport unloading relief planes in pitch darkness under fairly constant air bombardment and getting home
at seven every morning to sleep for two hours. He waved
our praises aside saying he only did it on alternate weeks.
"After tonight I can have my beauty sleep for seven
whole days."

His sitting-room reeked of stock fish, powdered milk,
powdered egg yolk and other relief odours which together can make the air of a place uninhalable. Father
Doherty rubbed his eyes with the back of his hand and
said what could he do for us. But before either of us
could begin he got up sleepily and reached for a big
thermos flask atop an empty bookcase harbouring just
one tiny crucifix, and asked if we cared for coffee. We
said yes thinking that in this very home and citadel of

Caritas whose very air reeked solid relief one could be sure that coffee would mean with sugar and milk. And I thought too that we were doing excellently with Father Doherty and set it down to our earlier politic admiration of his dedication and courage in the service of our people, for although he had seemed to wave it aside, judicious praise (if not flattery) was still a weapon which even saints might be vulnerable to. He disappeared into a room and brought back three mean-looking fading-blue plastic cups and poured the coffee, a little on his little finger first, into the cups apologising for the incompetence of his old flask.

I began politely to swallow mine and watched Cletus with the corner of my eye. He took a little birdlike sip and held it in his mouth.

Now, what could he do for us, asked Father Doherty again covering three quarters of an enormous yawn with the back of his hand. I spoke up first. I had problem with hay fever and would like some antihistamine tablets if he had any in stock. Certainly, he said, most certainly. "I have the very thing for you. Father Joseph has the same complaint, so I always keep some." He disappeared again and I could hear him saying: "Hay fever, hay fever, hay fever" like a man looking for a title in a well-stocked bookshelf, and then: "There we are!" Soon he emerged with a small bottle. "Everything here is in German," he said, studying the label with a squint. "Do you read German?"

"No."

"Nor do I. Try taking one thrice daily and see how you feel."

"Thank you, Father."

"Next!" he said jovially.

His short absence to get the tablets had enabled Cletus to transfer most of the coffee from his cup to his mouth and, moving smartly to the low window behind him and putting out his neck, disgorge it quickly outside.

"Name your wish. Joost wun wish, remember," said Father Doherty, now really gay.

"Father," said Cletus almost solemnly, "I need a little sugar."

I had been worrying since we got here how he was going to put that request across, what form of words he would use. Now it came out so pure and so simple like naked truth from the soul. I admired him for that performance for I knew I could never have managed it. Perhaps Father Doherty himself had unconsciously assisted by lending the circumstance, albeit jovially, a stark mythological simplicity. If so he now demolished it just as quickly and thoroughly as a capricious child might kick back into sand the magic castle he had just created. He seized Cletus by the scruff of his neck and shouting wretch! wretch! shoved him outside. Then he went for me; but I had already found and taken another exit. He raved and swore and stamped like a truly demented man. He prayed God to remember this outrage against His Holy Ghost on Judgement Day. Sugar! Sugar!! Sugar!!! he screamed in hoarse crescendo. Sugar when thousands of God's innocents perished daily for lack of a glass of milk! Worked up now beyond endurance by his own words he rushed out and made for us. And there was nothing for it but run, his holy imprecations ringing in our ears.

We spent a miserable, tongue-tied hour at the road junction trying to catch a lift back to Amafo. In the end we walked the ten miles again but now in the withering heat and fear of midday air raid.

That was one story that Cletus presumably wanted me to tell to celebrate our first tea party. How could I? I couldn't see it as victory in retrospect, only as defeat. And there were many, the ugliest yet to come.

Not long after our encounter with Father Doherty I was selected by the Foreign Affairs people "to go on a mission." Although it was a kind of poor man's mission lasting just a week and taking me no farther than the offshore Portuguese island of São Tomé I was nevertheless overjoyed because abroad was still abroad and I had never stepped out of Biafra since the war began—a fact calculated to dismiss one outright in the opinion of his fellows as a man of no consequence, but more important, which meant that one never had a chance to bask in the glory of coming back with those little amenities that had suddenly become marks of rank and good living, like bath soap, a towel, razor blades, etc.

On the last day before my journey, close friends and friends not so close, mere acquaintances and even complete strangers and near enemies came to tell me their wishes. It had become a ritual, almost a festival whose ancient significance was now buried deep in folk memory. Some lucky fellow was going on a mission to an almost mythical world long withdrawn beyond normal

human reach where goods abounded still and life was
safe. And everyone came to make their wishes. And to
every request the lucky one answered: "I will try, you
know the problem . . ."

"Oh yes I know, but just try . . ." No real hope, no
obligation or commitment.

Occasionally, however, a firm and serious order was
made when one of the happier people came. For this,
words were superfluous. Just a slip of paper with "foreign
exchange" pinned to it. Some wanted salt which was entirely out because of the weight. Many wanted an un-
derwear for themselves or their girls and some wretch
even ordered contraceptives which I told him I as-
sumed was for office (as against family) planning, to the
great amusement of my crowd. I bustled in and out of
my room gaily with my notepaper saying: Joost wun
wish!

Yes, near enemies came too. Like our big man across
the road, a one-time Protestant clergyman they said, now
unfrocked, a pompous ass if ever there was one, who
had early in the war wangled himself into the venal po-
sition of controlling and dispensing scarce materials
imported by the government, especially women's fabrics.
He came like a Nichodemus as I was about to turn in.
I wouldn't have thought he knew the likes of us existed.
But there he came nodding in his walk like an emir on
horseback and trailing the aroma of his Erinmore
tobacco. He wondered if I could buy him two bottles
of a special pomade for dying grey hair and held out a
five-dollar bill. This was the wretch who once asked my
girl friend when she went to file an application to buy a

bra to spend a weekend with him in some remote
village!

By foregoing lunch daily in São Tomé I was able at
the end of the week to save up from my miserable al-
lowance enough foreign exchange to buy myself a few
things including those antihistamine tablets (for I had
abandoned in our hasty retreat the bottle that Father
Doherty gave me). For Cletus—and this gave me the
greatest happiness of all—I bought a tin of Lipton's tea
and two half-pound packets of sugar. Imagine then my
horrified fury when one of the packets was stolen on my
arrival home at the airport while (my eyes turned mo-
mentarily away from my baggage) I was put through
make-believe immigration. Perhaps if that packet had
not been stolen Cletus might have been spared the most
humiliating defeat that sugar was yet to inflict on him.

Mercy came to see him (and me) the day I returned
from São Tomé. I had a tablet of Lux soap for her and a
small tube of hand cream. She was ecstatic.

"Would you like some tea?" asked Cletus.

"Oh yes," she said in her soft, purring voice. "Do you
have tea? Great! And sugar too! Great! Great! I must
take some."

I wasn't watching but I think she thrust her hand into
the opened packet of sugar and grabbed a handful and
was about to put it into her handbag. Cletus dropped
the kettle of hot water he was bringing in and pounced
on her. *That* I saw clearly. For a brief while she must
have thought it was some kind of grotesque joke. I knew
it wasn't and in that moment I came very near to loath-

ing him. He seized her hand containing the sugar and
began to prize it open, his teeth clenched.

"Stop it, Cletus!" I said.

"Stop, my arse," he said. "I am sick and tired of all
these grab-grab girls."

"Leave me alone," she cried, sudden tears of anger
and shame now running down her face. Somehow she
succeeded in wrenching her hand free. Then she stepped
back and threw the sugar full in his face, snatched her
handbag and ran away, crying. He picked up the sugar,
about half-a-dozen cubes.

"Sam!" shouted Cletus across to his houseboy. "Put some
more water on the fire." And then turning to me he said
again, his eyes glazed in crazy reminiscence: "Mike, you
must tell them the battle I waged with sugar."

"He was called Sugar Baby at school," I said, dodging
again.

"Oh, Mike, you're no bloody good with stories. I wonder who ever recommended you for the Propaganda
Directorate." The other two laughed. Beads of perspira-
tion trembled on his forehead. He was desperate. He was
on heat begging, pleading, touting for the sumptuous
agony of flagellation.

"And he lost his girl friend," I said turning brutal. "Yes,
he lost a nice, decent girl because he wouldn't part with
half-a-dozen cubes of the sugar I bought him."

"You know that's not fair," he said turning on me
sharply. "Nice girl indeed! Mercy was just a shameless
grabber like all the rest of them."

"Like all the rest of us. What interests me, Cletus, is

that you didn't find out all those months you went with
her and slept with her until I brought you a packet of
sugar. Then your eyes were opened."

"We know *you* brought it, Mike. You've told us already.
But that's not the point . . ."

"What then is the point?" Then I realized how foolish
it was and how easy, even now, to slip back into those
sudden irrational acrimonies of our recent desperate
days when an angry word dropping in unannounced
would start a fierce war like the passage of Esun between
two peace-loving friends. So I steered myself to a retrieving joke, retrieving albeit with a razor edge.

"When Cletus is ready to marry," I said, "they will have
to devise a special marriage vow for him. With all my
worldly goods—except my Tate and Lyle—I thee honour.
Father Doherty if they ever let him back in the country
will no doubt understand."

Umera and his friend laughed again.

GIRLS AT WAR

THE FIRST TIME their paths crossed nothing happened. That was in the first heady days of warlike preparation when thousands of young men (and sometimes women too) were daily turned away from enlistment centres because far too many of them were coming forward burning with readiness to bear arms in defence of the exciting new nation.

The second time they met was at a check-point at Awka. Then the war had started and was slowly moving southwards from the distant northern sector. He was driving from Onitsha to Enugu and was in a hurry. Although intellectually he approved of thorough searches at road-blocks, emotionally he was always offended whenever he had to submit to them. He would probably not admit it but the feeling people got was that if you were put through a search then you could not really be one of the big people. Generally he got away without a search by pronouncing in his deep, authoritative voice: "Reginald Nwankwo, Ministry of Justice." That almost always did it. But sometimes either through ignorance or sheer cussedness the crowd at the odd check-point would refuse to be impressed. As happened now at Awka. Two constables carrying heavy Mark 4 rifles were watching distantly from the roadside leaving the actual searching to local vigilantes.

"I am in a hurry," he said to the girl who now came up to his car. "My name is Reginald Nwankwo, Ministry of Justice."

"Good afternoon, sir. I want to see your boot."

"Oh Christ! What do you think is in the boot?"

"I don't know, sir."

He got out of the car in suppressed rage, stalked to the back, opened the boot and holding the lid up with his left hand he motioned with the right as if to say: After you!

"Are you satisfied?" he demanded.

"Yes, sir. Can I see your pigeon-hole?"

"Christ Almighty!"

"Sorry to delay you, sir. But you people gave us this job to do."

"Never mind. You are damn right. It's just that I happen to be in a hurry. But never mind. That's the glove-box. Nothing there as you can see."

"All right sir, close it." Then she opened the rear door and bent down to inspect under the seats. It was then he took the first real look at her, starting from behind. She was a beautiful girl in a breasty blue jersey, khaki jeans and canvas shoes with the new-style hair-plait which gave a girl a defiant look and which they called— for reasons of their own—"air force base"; and she looked vaguely familiar.

"I am all right, sir," she said at last meaning she was through with her task. "You don't recognize me?"

"No. Should I?"

"You gave me a lift to Enugu that time I left my school to go and join the militia."

"Ah, yes, you were the girl. I told you, didn't I, to go back to school because girls were not required in the militia. What happened?"

"They told me to go back to my school or join the Red Cross."

"You see I was right. So, what are you doing now?"

"Just patching up with Civil Defence."

"Well, good luck to you. Believe me you are a great girl."

That was the day he finally believed there might be something in this talk about revolution. He had seen plenty of girls and women marching and demonstrating before now. But somehow he had never been able to give it much thought. He didn't doubt that the girls and the women took themselves seriously; they obviously did. But so did the little kids who marched up and down the streets at the time drilling with sticks and wearing their mothers' soup bowls for steel helmets. The prime joke of the time among his friends was the contingent of girls

from a local secondary school marching behind a banner:
WE ARE IMPREGNABLE!

But after that encounter at the Awka check-point he
simply could not sneer at the girls again, nor at the talk
of revolution, for he had seen it in action in that young
woman whose devotion had simply and without self-
righteousness convicted him of gross levity. What were
her words? We are doing the work you asked us to do.
She wasn't going to make an exception even for one who
once did her a favour. He was sure she would have
searched her own father just as rigorously.

When their paths crossed a third time, at least eighteen
months later, things had got very bad. Death and starva-
tion having long chased out the headiness of the early
days, now left in some places blank resignation, in others a
rock-like, even suicidal, defiance. But surprisingly enough
there were many at this time also who had no other
desire than to corner whatever good things were still going and to enjoy themselves to the limit. For such people a strange normalcy had returned to the world. All
those nervous check-points disappeared. Girls became
girls once more and boys boys. It was a tight, blockaded
and desperate world but none the less a world—with some
goodness and some badness and plenty of heroism which,
however, happened most times far, far below the eye-
level of the people in this story—in out-of-the-way
refugee camps, in the damp tatters, in the hungry and
bare-handed courage of the first line of fire.

Reginald Nwankwo lived in Owerri then. But that day
he had gone to Nkwerri in search of relief. He had got
from Caritas in Owerri a few heads of stock-fish, some

tinned meat, and the dreadful American stuff called For-
mula Two which he felt certain was some kind of animal
feed. But he always had a vague suspicion that not being
a Catholic put one at a disadvantage with Caritas. So
he went now to see an old friend who ran the WCC depot
at Nkwerri to get other items like rice, beans and that
excellent cereal commonly called Gabon gari.

He left Owerri at six in the morning so as to catch
his friend at the depot where he was known never to
linger beyond 8.30 for fear of air-raids. Nwankwo was
very fortunate that day. The depot had received on the
previous day large supplies of new stock as a result of an
unusual number of plane landings a few nights earlier.
As his driver loaded tins and bags and cartons into his
car the starved crowds that perpetually hung around relief centres made crude, ungracious remarks like "War
Can Continue!" meaning the WCC! Somebody else
shouted "Irevolu!" and his friends replied "shum!" "Irevolu!" "shum!" "Isofeli?" "shum!" "Isofeli?" "Mba!"

Nwankwo was deeply embarrassed not by the jeers of
this scarecrow crowd of rags and floating ribs but by the
independent accusation of their wasted bodies and
sunken eyes. Indeed he would probably have felt much
worse had they said nothing, simply looked on in silence,
as his boot was loaded with milk, and powdered egg and
oats and tinned meat and stock-fish. By nature such singu-
lar good fortune in the midst of a general desolation was
certain to embarrass him. But what could a man do? He
had a wife and four children living in the remote village
of Ogbu and completely dependent on what relief he
could find and send them. He couldn't abandon them

to kwashiokor. The best he could do—and did do as a matter of fact—was to make sure that whenever he got sizeable supplies like now he made over some of it to his driver, Johnson, with a wife and six, or was it seven? children and a salary of ten pounds a month when gari in the market was climbing to one pound per cigarette cup. In such a situation one could do nothing at all for crowds; at best one could try to be of some use to one's immediate neighbours. That was all.

On his way back to Owerri a very attractive girl by the roadside waved for a lift. He ordered the driver to stop. Scores of pedestrians, dusty and exhausted, some military, some civil, swooped down on the car from all directions.

"No, no, no," said Nwankwo firmly. "It's the young woman I stopped for. I have a bad tyre and can only take one person. Sorry."

"My son, please," cried one old woman in despair, gripping the door-handle.

"Old woman, you want to be killed?" shouted the driver as he pulled away, shaking her off. Nwankwo had already opened a book and sunk his eyes there. For at least a mile after that he did not even look at the girl until she finding, perhaps, the silence too heavy said:

"You've saved me today. Thank you."

"Not at all. Where are you going?"

"To Owerri. You don't recognize me?"

"Oh yes, of course. What a fool I am . . . You are . . ."

"Gladys."

"That's right, the militia girl. You've changed, Gladys.

You were always beautiful of course, but now you are a beauty queen. What do you do these days?"

"I am in the Fuel Directorate."

"That's wonderful."

It was wonderful, he thought, but even more it was tragic. She wore a high-tinted wig and a very expensive skirt and low-cut blouse. Her shoes, obviously from Gabon, must have cost a fortune. In short, thought Nwankwo, she had to be in the keep of some well-placed gentleman, one of those piling up money out of the war.

"I broke my rule today to give you a lift. I never give lifts these days."

"Why?"

"How many people can you carry? It is better not to try at all. Look at that old woman."

"I thought you would carry her."

He said nothing to that and after another spell of silence Gladys thought maybe he was offended and so added: "Thank you for breaking your rule for me." She was scanning his face, turned slightly away. He smiled, turned, and tapped her on the lap.

"What are you going to Owerri to do?"

"I am going to visit my girl friend."

"Girl friend? You sure?"

"Why not? . . . If you drop me at her house you can see her. Only I pray God she hasn't gone on weekend today; it will be serious."

"Why?"

"Because if she is not at home I will sleep on the road today."

"I pray to God that she is not at home."

"Why?"

"Because if she is not at home I will offer you bed and breakfast . . . What is that?" he asked the driver who had brought the car to an abrupt stop. There was no need for an answer. The small crowd ahead was looking upwards. The three scrambled out of the car and stumbled for the bush, necks twisted in a backward search of the sky. But the alarm was false. The sky was silent and clear except for two high-flying vultures. A humorist in the crowd called them Fighter and Bomber and everyone laughed in relief. The three climbed into their car again and continued their journey.

"It is much too early for raids," he said to Gladys, who had both her palms on her breast as though to still a thumping heart. "They rarely come before ten o'clock."

But she remained tongue-tied from her recent fright. Nwankwo saw an opportunity there and took it at once.

"Where does your friend live?"

"250 Douglas Road."

"Ah! that's the very centre of town—a terrible place. No bunkers, nothing. I won't advise you to go there before 6 p.m.; it's not safe. If you don't mind I will take you to my place where there is a good bunker and then as soon as it is safe, around six, I shall drive you to your friend. How's that?"

"It's all right," she said lifelessly. "I am so frightened of this thing. That's why I refused to work in Owerri. I don't even know who asked me to come out today."

"You'll be all right. We are used to it."

"But your family is not there with you?"

"No," he said. "Nobody has his family there. We like

to say it is because of air-raids but I can assure you there is more to it. Owerri is a real swinging town and we live the life of gay bachelors."

"That is what I have heard."

"You will not just hear it; you will see it today. I shall take you to a real swinging party. A friend of mine, a Lieutenant-Colonel, is having a birthday party. He's hired the Sound Smashers to play. I'm sure you'll enjoy it."

He was immediately and thoroughly ashamed of himself. He hated the parties and frivolities to which his friends clung like drowning men. And to talk so approvingly of them because he wanted to take a girl home! And this particular girl too, who had once had such beautiful faith in the struggle and was betrayed (no doubt about it) by some man like him out for a good time. He shook his head sadly.

"What is it?" asked Gladys.

"Nothing. Just my thoughts."

They made the rest of the journey to Owerri practically in silence.

She made herself at home very quickly as if she was a regular girl friend of his. She changed into a house dress and put away her auburn wig.

"That is a lovely hair-do. Why do you hide it with a wig?"

"Thank you," she said leaving his question unanswered for a while. Then she said: "Men are funny."

"Why do you say that?"

"You are now a beauty queen," she mimicked.

"Oh, that! I mean every word of it." He pulled her to

him and kissed her. She neither refused nor yielded fully,
which he liked for a start. Too many girls were simply
too easy those days. War sickness, some called it.

He drove off a little later to look in at the office and
she busied herself in the kitchen helping his boy with
lunch. It must have been literally a look-in, for he was
back within half an hour, rubbing his hands and saying
he could not stay away too long from his beauty queen.

As they sat down to lunch she said: "You have nothing
in your fridge."

"Like what?" he asked, half-offended.

"Like meat," she replied undaunted.

"Do you still eat meat?" he challenged.

"Who am I? But other big men like you eat."

"I don't know which big men you have in mind. But
they are not like me. I don't make money trading with
the enemy or selling relief or . . ."

"Augusta's boy friend doesn't do that. He just gets foreign exchange."

"How does he get it? He swindles the government—
that's how he gets foreign exchange, whoever he is. Who
is Augusta, by the way?"

"My girl friend."

"I see."

"She gave me three dollars last time which I changed
to forty-five pounds. The man gave her fifty dollars."

"Well, my dear girl, I don't traffic in foreign exchange
and I don't have meat in my fridge. We are fighting a
war and I happen to know that some young boys at the
front drink gari and water once in three days."

"It is true," she said simply. "Monkey de work, baboon de chop."

"It is not even that; it is worse," he said, his voice beginning to shake. "People are dying every day. As we talk now somebody is dying."

"It is true," she said again.

"Plane!" screamed his boy from the kitchen.

"My mother!" screamed Gladys. As they scuttled towards the bunker of palm stems and red earth, covering their heads with their hands and stooping slightly in their flight, the entire sky was exploding with the clamour of jets and the huge noise of homemade anti-aircraft rockets.

Inside the bunker she clung to him even after the plane had gone and the guns, late to start and also to end, had all died down again.

"It was only passing," he told her, his voice a little shaky. "It didn't drop anything. From its direction I should say it was going to the war front. Perhaps our people are pressing them. That's what they always do. Whenever our boys press them, they send an SOS to the Russians and Egyptians to bring the planes." He drew a long breath.

She said nothing, just clung to him. They could hear his boy telling the servant from the next house that there were two of them and one dived like this and the other dived like that.

"I see dem well well," said the other with equal excitement. "If no to say de ting de kill porson e for sweet for eye. To God."

"Imagine!" said Gladys, finding her voice at last. She

had a way, he thought, of conveying with a few words
or even a single word whole layers of meaning. Now it
was at once her astonishment as well as reproof, tinged
perhaps with grudging admiration for people who could
be so light-hearted about these bringers of death.

"Don't be so scared," he said. She moved closer and
he began to kiss her and squeeze her breasts. She yielded
more and more and then fully. The bunker was dark and
unswept and might harbour crawling things. He thought
of bringing a mat from the main house but reluctantly
decided against it. Another plane might pass and send a
neighbour or simply a chance passer-by crashing into
them. That would be only slightly better than a certain
gentleman in another air-raid who was seen in broad daylight fleeing his bedroom for his bunker stark-naked pursued by a woman in a similar state!

Just as Gladys had feared, her friend was not in town.
It would seem her powerful boy friend had wangled for
her a flight to Libreville to shop. So her neighbours
thought anyway.

"Great!" said Nwankwo as they drove away. "She will
come back on an arms plane loaded with shoes, wigs,
pants, bras, cosmetics and what have you, which she will
then sell and make thousands of pounds. You girls are
really at war, aren't you?"

She said nothing and he thought he had got through
at last to her. Then suddenly she said, "That is what you
men want us to do."

"Well," he said, "here is one man who doesn't want you

to do that. Do you remember that girl in khaki jeans who searched me without mercy at the check-point?"

She began to laugh.

"That is the girl I want you to become again. Do you remember her? No wig. I don't even think she had any earrings . . ."

"Ah, na lie-o. I had earrings."

"All right. But you know what I mean."

"That time done pass. Now everybody want survival. They call it number six. You put your number six; I put my number six. Everything all right."

The Lieutenant-Colonel's party turned into something quite unexpected. But before it did things had been going well enough. There was goat-meat, some chicken and rice and plenty of home-made spirits. There was one fiery brand nicknamed "tracer" which indeed sent a flame down your gullet. The funny thing was looking at it in the bottle it had the innocent appearance of an orange drink. But the thing that caused the greatest stir was the bread—one little roll for each person! It was the size of a golf-ball and about the same consistency too! But it was real bread. The band was good too and there were many girls. And to improve matters even further two white Red Cross people soon arrived with a bottle of Courvoisier and a bottle of Scotch! The party gave them a standing ovation and then scrambled to get a taste. It soon turned out from his general behaviour, however, that one of the white men had probably drunk too much already. And the reason it would seem was that a pilot he knew well had been killed in a crash at the airport last night, flying in relief in awful weather.

Few people at the party had heard of the crash by then. So there was an immediate damping of the air. Some dancing couples went back to their seats and the band stopped. Then for some strange reason the drunken Red Cross man just exploded.

"Why should a man, a decent man, throw away his life. For nothing! Charley didn't need to die. Not for this stinking place. Yes, everything stinks here. Even these girls who come here all dolled up and smiling, what are they worth? Don't I know? A head of stock-fish, that's all, or one American dollar and they are ready to tumble into bed."

In the threatening silence following the explosion one of the young officers walked up to him and gave him three thundering slaps—right! left! right!—pulled him up from his seat and (there were things like tears in his eyes) shoved him outside. His friend, who had tried in vain to shut him up, followed him out and the silenced party heard them drive off. The officer who did the job returned dusting his palms.

"Fucking beast!" said he with an impressive coolness. And all the girls showed with their eyes that they rated him a man and a hero.

"Do you know him?" Gladys asked Nwankwo.

He didn't answer her. Instead he spoke generally to the party:

"The fellow was clearly drunk," he said.

"I don't care," said the officer. "It is when a man is drunk that he speaks what is on his mind."

"So you beat him for what was on his mind," said the host, "that is the spirit, Joe."

"Thank you, sir," said Joe, saluting.

"His name is Joe," Gladys and the girl on her left said in unison, turning to each other.

At the same time Nwankwo and a friend on the other side of him were saying quietly, very quietly, that although the man had been rude and offensive what he had said about the girls was unfortunately the bitter truth, only he was the wrong man to say it.

When the dancing resumed Captain Joe came to Gladys for a dance. She sprang to her feet even before the word was out of his mouth. Then she remembered immediately and turned round to take permission from Nwankwo. At the same time the Captain also turned to him and said, "Excuse me."

"Go ahead," said Nwankwo, looking somewhere between the two.

It was a long dance and he followed them with his eyes without appearing to do so. Occasionally a relief plane passed overhead and somebody immediately switched off the lights saying it might be the Intruder. But it was only an excuse to dance in the dark and make the girls giggle, for the sound of the Intruder was well known.

Gladys came back feeling very self-conscious and asked Nwankwo to dance with her. But he wouldn't. "Don't bother about me," he said, "I am enjoying myself perfectly sitting here and watching those of you who dance."

"Then let's go," she said, "if you won't dance."

"But I never dance, believe me. So please enjoy yourself."

She danced next with the Lieutenant-Colonel and again with Captain Joe, and then Nwankwo agreed to take her home.

"I am sorry I didn't dance," he said as they drove away. "But I swore never to dance as long as this war lasts."

She said nothing.

"When I think of somebody like that pilot who got killed last night. And he had no hand whatever in the quarrel. All his concern was to bring us food . . ."

"I hope that his friend is not like him," said Gladys.

"The man was just upset by his friend's death. But what I am saying is that with people like that getting killed and our own boys suffering and dying at the war fronts I don't see why we should sit around throwing parties and dancing."

"You took me there," said she in final revolt. "They are your friends. I don't know them before."

"Look, my dear, I am not blaming you. I am merely telling you why I personally refuse to dance. Anyway, let's change the subject . . . Do you still say you want to go back tomorrow? My driver can take you early enough on Monday morning for you to go to work. No? All right, just as you wish. You are the boss."

She gave him a shock by the readiness with which she followed him to bed and by her language.

"You want to shell?" she asked. And without waiting for an answer said, "Go ahead but don't pour in troops!"

He didn't want to pour in troops either and so it was

all right. But she wanted visual assurance and so he showed her.

One of the ingenious economies taught by the war was that a rubber condom could be used over and over again. All you had to do was wash it out, dry it and shake a lot of talcum powder over it to prevent its sticking; and it was as good as new. It had to be the real British thing, though, not some of the cheap stuff they brought in from Lisbon which was about as strong as a dry cocoyam leaf in the harmattan.

He had his pleasure but wrote the girl off. He might just as well have slept with a prostitute, he thought. It was clear as daylight to him now that she was kept by some army officer. What a terrible transformation in the short period of less than two years! Wasn't it a miracle that she still had memories of the other life, that she even remembered her name? If the affair of the drunken Red Cross man should happen again now, he said to himself, he would stand up beside the fellow and tell the party that here was a man of truth. What a terrible fate to be-fall a whole generation! The mothers of tomorrow!

By morning he was feeling a little better and more generous in his judgements. Gladys, he thought, was just a mirror reflecting a society that had gone completely rotten and maggotty at the centre. The mirror itself was intact; a lot of smudge but no more. All that was needed was a clean duster. "I have a duty to her," he told himself, "the little girl that once revealed to me our situation. Now she is in danger, under some terrible influence."

He wanted to get to the bottom of this deadly influence. It was clearly not just her good-time girl friend,

Augusta, or whatever her name was. There must be some man at the centre of it, perhaps one of these heartless attack-traders who traffic in foreign currencies and make their hundreds of thousands by sending young men to hazard their lives bartering looted goods for cigarettes behind enemy lines, or one of those contractors who receive piles of money daily for food they never deliver to the army. Or perhaps some vulgar and cowardly army officer full of filthy barrack talk and fictitious stories of heroism. He decided he had to find out. Last night he had thought of sending his driver alone to take her home. But no, he must go and see for himself where she lived. Something was bound to reveal itself there. Something on which he could anchor his saving operation. As he prepared for the trip his feeling towards her softened with every passing minute. He assembled for her half of the food he had received at the relief centre the day before. Difficult as things were, he thought, a girl who had something to eat would be spared, not all, but some of the temptation. He would arrange with his friend at the WCC to deliver something to her every fortnight.

Tears came to Gladys's eyes when she saw the gifts. Nwankwo didn't have too much cash on him but he got together twenty pounds and handed it over to her.

"I don't have foreign exchange, and I know this won't go far at all, but . . ."

She just came and threw herself at him, sobbing. He kissed her lips and eyes and mumbled something about victims of circumstance, which went over her head. In deference to him, he thought with exultation, she had put away her high-tinted wig in her bag.

"I want you to promise me something," he said.

"What?"

"Never use that expression about shelling again."

She smiled with tears in her eyes. "You don't like it? That's what all the girls call it."

"Well, you are different from all the girls. Will you promise?"

"O.K."

Naturally their departure had become a little delayed. And when they got into the car it refused to start. After poking around the engine the driver decided that the battery was flat. Nwankwo was aghast. He had that very week paid thirty-four pounds to change two of the cells and the mechanic who performed it had promised him six months' service. A new battery, which was then running at two hundred and fifty pounds was simply out of the question. The driver must have been careless with something, he thought.

"It must be because of last night," said the driver.

"What happened last night?" asked Nwankwo sharply, wondering what insolence was on the way. But none was intended.

"Because we use the head light."

"Am I supposed not to use my light then? Go and get some people and try pushing it." He got out again with Gladys and returned to the house while the driver went over to neighbouring houses to seek the help of other servants.

After at least half an hour of pushing it up and down the street, and a lot of noisy advice from the pushers, the

car finally spluttered to life shooting out enormous clouds
of black smoke from the exhaust.

It was eight-thirty by his watch when they set out. A
few miles away a disabled soldier waved for a lift.

"Stop!" screamed Nwankwo. The driver jammed his
foot on the brakes and then turned his head towards his
master in bewilderment.

"Don't you see the soldier waving? Reverse and pick
him up!"

"Sorry, sir," said the driver. "I don't know Master wan
to pick him."

"If you don't know you should ask. Reverse back."

The soldier, a mere boy, in filthy khaki drenched in
sweat lacked his right leg from the knee down. He
seemed not only grateful that a car should stop for him
but greatly surprised. He first handed in his crude
wooden crutches which the driver arranged between the
two front seats, then painfully he levered himself in.

"Thank sir," he said turning his neck to look at the back
and completely out of breath.

"I am very grateful. Madame, thank you."

"The pleasure is ours," said Nwankwo. "Where did you
get your wound?"

"At Azumini, sir. On tenth of January."

"Never mind. Everything will be all right. We are
proud of you boys and will make sure you receive your
due reward when it is all over."

"I pray God, sir."

They drove on in silence for the next half-hour or so.
Then as the car sped down a slope towards a bridge
somebody screamed—perhaps the driver, perhaps the

soldier—"They have come!" The screech of the brakes
merged into the scream and the shattering of the sky
overhead. The doors flew open even before the car had
come to a stop and they were fleeing blindly to the bush.
Gladys was a little ahead of Nwankwo when they heard
through the drowning tumult the soldier's voice crying:
"Please come and open for me!" Vaguely he saw Gladys
stop; he pushed past her shouting to her at the same time
to come on. Then a high whistle descended like a spear
through the chaos and exploded in a vast noise and mo-
tion that smashed up everything. A tree he had embraced
flung him away through the bush. Then another terrible
whistle starting high up and ending again in a monumental crash of the world; and then another, and
Nwankwo heard no more.

He woke up to human noises and weeping and the
smell and smoke of a charred world. He dragged himself
up and staggered towards the source of the sounds.

From afar he saw his driver running towards him in
tears and blood. He saw the remains of his car smoking
and the entangled remains of the girl and the soldier.
And he let out a piercing cry and fell down again.